Stories from the World of Tomorrow

The Way the Future Was!

Edited by
Andrew MacRae

DARKHOUSE BOOKS

Stories from the World of Tomorrow
All rights reserved

These are works of fiction. Any resemblance between events, places, or characters, within them, and actual events, organizations, or people, is but happenstance.

No part of this book may be reproduced or transmitted in any form or by any means, electronic or mechanical, including photocopying, recording, or by any information storage and retrieval system, without permission in writing from the publisher.

Published July, 2015

Published in the United States of America

Darkhouse Books
160 J Street, #2223
Niles, California 94539

Introduction

"To its visitors the Fair will say: "Here are the materials, ideas, and forces at work in our world. These are the tools with which the World of Tomorrow must be made."
—New York World's Fair pamphlet

Worlds ending and worlds beginning are common themes in speculative fiction. Within our local time-space continuum, the year of 1939 marked both the end of one world and the start of another. The last, lingering vestiges of the Victorian and Edwardian eras disappeared as a second world war drove a technological revolution that was, in scale and pace, greater than any known to history.

The 1939 New York World's Fair is symbolic of the pervasive, precarious, and mostly pessimistic mood that held the world in its grip. War was coming. War was inevitable. Fighting had already broken out in a dozen spots around the globe. Particularly poignant were the countries whose exhibits closed as their mother countries disappeared, Poland, Belgium, and Czechoslovakia among them. The fair closed in 1940 and many of the nationals from countries overrun by war were unable to return home, and instead settled in the US.

Yet the 1939 fair is also emblematic of the indomitable optimism that characterizes our species. The future was on display and millions of people were enticed, entranced, and encouraged by the promise of that future. Enormous dioramas displayed models of gleaming skyways and illuminated highways crossing the continent. Mechanical marvels marched, for a step or two, on stage, and conversed with an astonished audience.

The fiction in this anthology explores that future, yet it cannot help but be shaped by the realities that have transpired in the nearly four-score years since the fair closed. Robots you will find, and rockets, too. But you will also discover musings and explorations into the consequences such inventions might engender. The story of Pandora and the forbidden container may be an archetypical myth, but the reason it and other ancient myths exist, is because there is truth at the heart of each. The authors of the play *"Inherit the Wind"*, Jerome Lawrence and Robert E. Lee, expressed this truth well, when Henry Drummond reflects on progress and its cost, ending with, *"Mister, you may conquer the air; but the birds will lose their wonder, and the clouds will smell of gasoline."*

There is, perhaps, no better way with which to conclude this introduction but with a phrase coined by the late, great science fiction author and editor, Lester del Ray, a favorite of mine when I was young and discovering worlds of wonder, and a favorite today as I begin to reflect back on my life. It is a phrase that sums up the theme of this book best:

The way the future was.

Andrew MacRae
July, 2015
Niles, California

We lead off our anthology with a story by Amanda Bergloff. Ms Bergloff tells us the theme of this story was inspired by the research she did on the General Motors Futurama Diorama at the 1939 World's Fair.

She is a writer and illustrator for the ongoing graphic novel anthology, "Crimson Dreams", published by ACME Comics. She is also an editor and feature writer for "The House of Mystery: Comics and More" website.

Artificial Girls on the Illuminated Highway

By Amanda Bergloff

It was their eyes that got to me. Everyone stood around my screen laughing, except me. It was the lifeless look in their eyes that were trying desperately to look human, when bits of light reflected in them, that made me feel sad.

I was a research assistant at Jeeyem and was asked to find archival photos and footage for a presentation the company was putting together for the upcoming city centennial called, "Dawn of a New Day: A Celebration of Safety and Efficiency." Jeeyem's presentation would showcase the progress the company made in the fields of robotics and transportation. In a future that can be whatever we propose to make it, Jeeyem strived to replace the old with new ideas and technology.

I spent the morning going through images and videos, and my eyes hurt from staring at the screen for hours without a break. I finally found an interesting picture of something called, "The Ghost Car", which was a transparent car made from clear plexiglass that was featured at some kind of special fair many years ago. It was a beautiful work of art that showed the inner workings of something we take for granted every day. I was fascinated by the idea of the mechanical interior works being visible in the form of this car and I looked back in time to the world it was created in. I found an idealistic manifesto someone had written about their view of what the future promised for the fair that year, and I copied much of the text, thinking I could use quotes from it during my portion of the presentation.

This world of tomorrow is a world of beauty…

While I was looking through more of the old fair footage, a video came across my screen with the title, "Artificial Girls". There, suddenly in front of me in full color, were two full sized female robots. There was no sound that went with the images, so it was odd to see each of them standing in silence on their own little balcony, overlooking crowds of people, dressed in the strange clothing of the day, with their hips making circular movements like a bored exotic dancer. Their sheer tops made their plastic nipples visible.

What got to me though, were their faces. Unlike the Ghost Car that was completely transparent, these Artificial Girls wore masks to cover their inner workings. The screen showed close ups of their strange, rubber faces, with eyes their makers obviously wanted to appear human, but instead looked blank, with a haunted stare that I couldn't turn away from.

It was also quite a statement to me that the idea of "womanhood" had been distilled down to gyrating hips and nipples, their makers believing that this was a representation that would be interesting to people of the day.

At the end of the clip, was another one about the other proto-robot on exhibit at the same fair. This clip was also in color, but this one had sound. On display was a large, gold colored, box-shaped male entity that made no attempt to look like a real human being, like the Artificial Girls did. He stood seven feet tall, weighed two hundred fifty pounds and proclaimed in a stilted, booming voice, "My brain is bigger than yours," and smoked cigarettes.

The women promised physical delights, while the male proclaimed his ego.

I kept re-playing the Artificial Girls part over and over. Someone walking by my screen stopped and laughed, and called some other co-workers over. They stood there laughing, while all I could think of was that the lifeless look in the dark eyes of the Artificial Girls resonated deep within me, and I didn't really know why.

I shut my screen off and waved the surrounding crowd away.

These ideas are all interesting and much effort has been expended to lay them before you in an interesting way...

I sat back in my chair after everyone left and thought about the weird and disturbing, yet strangely familiar faces of the Artificial Girls. I had a feeling I had seen them before, and it bothered me.

There was an elevated walk outside my third floor office. These elevated sidewalks made it possible to double the available width of traffic in the street below, so there were no more rush hour traffic problems.

I was separated by steel and mirrored glass from people walking less than ten feet away from me. I could see out, but they couldn't see in. I stared at them shuffling about, here and there with their rubber faces covering their interior workings.

I watched until the sun was at an angle that blinded my eyes. I blinked and for a second saw directly in front of me, that face. That same automaton face with lifeless eyes. My own reflection in the window. I stood up. I had to get out of there.

"Are you leaving already?" a co-worker asked.

"Yes, I finished early," I lied.

The co-worker continued, "Well I'll look for you on the screens tonight. Are you going to be updating your channel?"

"I don't know. I don't think I have anything new to say right now."

"Oh come on, of course you do. You could share that robot girl video you found. That's hilarious."

"Maybe."

"You don't have to be lonely, you know," the co-worker's autom-aton face called after me as I walked away.

Lonely? I'm not lonely. I just don't have time to look back.

We're all just waiting for the future to start…

I stepped onto the elevated sidewalk and breathed in the fresh air. I had no intention of being part of their conversations tonight… conversations that they put into the air in the hopes that someone will answer. I heard once that radio waves and thought go out for-ever, beyond our planet, beyond the stars. I hope not. Some things are not worth it.

I usually look around at the breathtaking architecture and smile at people as I walk ten city blocks to the monorail station, but today I just tried to avoid eye contact with the other pedestrians. All I could see were faces with the same, desperately trying to look human, eyes.

I sat by myself in the back of the monorail, next to the window. The setting sun infused the landscape with hyper-realistic, saturated color making the green parkways surrounding the circular airport and industrial and commercial sections of the city stand out. It was as though someone had taken a thick green marker and outlined those areas. I never really saw before how there was such a purposeful con-tinuity and proper placement of these city elements until now. I could see clearly that they were separated for greater efficiency and greater convenience for all, and I didn't think of eyes the whole ride home.

Space for living, space for working. All available for more people than ever before…

I couldn't sleep. Images wandered in my mind that I couldn't turn off. Transparent, Plexiglass thoughts, and eyes with pinpoints of light looking out from the shadows.

I felt the need to be out of the city and see the farm where I grew up. Everything was simpler then…before efficiency…before safety.

All the activities of science lead us onward to better methods of doing things…

My car enters the seven-lane highway at the same rate of speed as the other cars. The highway is always lit evenly by a bluish glow that comes from tubing located in each lane's safety curbing. It gives the illusion that the road is always straight.

Tonight, all I want to do is drive and see finally where the illuminated highway will take me. I don't want to see those eyes in my mind anymore. I won't turn around and look back.

A new world is constantly opening before us at an ever-accelerating rate of progress…

I cross the suspension bridge that leads out of the city and start feeling lighter. The bridge is a wonder of technology. I feel like I'm leaving the automatons behind.

The two lines of blue stretching out in front of me on the illuminated highway never change, but the surrounding landscape does. I pass an amusement park closed for the night. Its colorful life dimmed by the fluorescent after-hours lights of the cleanup crew.

Man's progress has brought more leisure for amusement and recreation, bringing them within easier reach of more people…

The landscape changes again as I enter a rural section. The blue glow of the highway glints off of the individual glass domes covering each tree in the orchard, giving it them a magical glow.

My dad told me when I was little, that there was no magic in the world, though. It was advancements in science that eliminated his worry about disease and insects on his farm. Scientists came to him one day and told him they could influence pollination by artificial feeding in his orchards and they installed the glass domes. Science had shortened his hours of work and gave him greater security in his daily life.

Physics and chemistry have joined hands in helpful friendship…

He died later that year. Science couldn't prevent that. My mom put the farm up for sale and we moved to the city.

On second thought, maybe life wasn't simpler on the farm.

Over space, man has begun to win victory…

The highway is playing tricks on my eyes now. I'm getting lost, but I know I'm going straight. I know if I just keep going straight, I will find my way.

I've passed the rural areas, and now I'm looking down on the valley and the aeration plant that purifies lake water for the inhabitants of the valley to use.

I hadn't realized I already climbed the a mountain with the religious retreat at the top and the resort town just on the other side.

We'll always find new things for all others to enjoy…

When I see the giant mountain lake dam ahead, it seems the deep blue of the lake is mingling with the blue of the highway. I hear the words in my head, "You don't have to be lonely, you know." I'm not sure if I'm still driving on the highway anymore. Ideas are fading.

It is but a symbol of a greater world… a better world… a world which always will grow forward…

I feel disconnected to my surroundings. I fear my eyes are glazing over and becoming less human. I'm running from something I can't prevent. I am an Artificial Girl at the horizon of my dreamscape.

I'm driving the Ghost Car, made of clear acrylic. The inner workings visible. I'm transparent, too, my organs replaced by gears and metal. All except for my heart. That, I can still feel beating inside of me. The one last, organic piece. I feel like I'm floating. I'm not sure where I am, and for a moment, I look back.

The suspension bridge is behind me and I've crossed back into the city, and from here, it looks like the city is sighing from its soul.

Perhaps this illuminated highway is an endless loop, circulating the madness of the beliefs we create for ourselves.

It's time to start another day. The city is determined to unfold constantly greater possibilities of tomorrow. It's all here…for everyone, as we move rapidly forward, because this is where we are going to spend the rest of our lives.

Tonight, I will again be on the illuminated highway, but this time I won't look back.

Several stories in our anthology make use of the robot created by Westinghouse Electric. While clumsy by modern standards, it was his image that came to mind for an entire generation who saw him perform at the World's Fair. In this story a young girl makes a friend for life when on a visit to the fair.

Mr. Rugg is the author of numerous science fiction stories as well as the non-fiction book, 'Rugg's Handbook of Sales and Science Fiction.

A Deep Breath of Tomorrow

By Raymond K. Rugg

One day in 1939, Myra began her journey toward the future.

That was the day she accompanied her father to the World's Fair. He was meeting with an old friend and colleague, Dr. Keeler, although Myra knew him as Uncle Bert. Keeler was a leading researcher in the field of electronics, in charge of the robotics exhibit at the Fair.

"Find a chair and sit quietly, dear, while Uncle Bert and I chat." The three of them were in an office behind Keeler's display where they crowded in among his paperwork and packing crates. It was a small space, made much smaller by the presence of the robot that was the centerpiece of his research, and of his exhibit.

"But Papa! Can't I go and see the—" and her voice went breathless with wonder—"the World of Tomorrow?"

"I'm afraid that even in the world of tomorrow, little five-year-old-girls can't wander about unchaperoned, sweetheart."

Uncle Bert spoke up. "Oh, let her go, Sammy." He reached down and pinched Myra's cheeks lovingly. "Every little girl deserves an adventure now and then. Look," he said, gesturing to his mechanical man, "my Electronico can accompany her, and she will be perfectly safe."

Father looked skeptical. "Yes, yes, your robot is an electronic marvel, Bert. But being able to differentiate between red and green, and being able to smoke a cigarette, these things hardly qualify your automaton to be a fit companion for a small child."

Uncle Bert chuckled. "Oh, most of that is just an act for the fair-goers! Electronico has the same mental capacity as you or me, and is learning all the time! Just watch!" He reached behind the robot and flipped a switch on its back.

A loud humming sound came from within the barrel chest. Spiral apertures slid open to reveal eye-lenses. A mechanical voice came from the mouth. "Hello... I... am... Elec... tronico... It... is... nice... to... meet... you."

"Ellie, enough with the mechano-man bit! These are my friends." Bert gestured to his visitors. "Ellie, meet Dr. Samuel Cohen, pre-eminent cardiologist, and his daughter, Myra, pre-eminent heartbreaker of the preschool set. Sam, Myra, meet Electronico, better known as Ellie to those of us in the robotics biz."

The robot's voice changed. Gone were the lifeless and mechanical intonations, replaced by a decidedly Brooklyn accent. "Whew, what a relief! You can't believe how boring it gets, having to play dumb for the rubes. Pleased ta meetcha, Doc." The robot shook hands with a dazed-looking Samuel Cohen, and then repeated the action with Myra. "How ya doin', cutie pie?" Myra was delighted and shook his hand with the same vigor as pumping a well-handle.

"And I am very pleased to meet you, as well, er, Ellie," Father replied politely. To his host, he commented, "So, Bert. Now I see perhaps why you wanted to speak with me."

"Oh, Sam, we have so much to talk about! Our progress in the field astounds even me! Yes, sit!" To the robot, "Ellie, would you be a pal and take Miss Cohen here around to see the fair?"

"You betcha, Doc. You don't have to ask me twice to take a stroll with the prettiest girl in town. Gimme a light, and then she and I will go see the sights." Uncle Bert lit a cigarette and placed it in the robot's metal fingers. Electronico raised it to his mouth and took a long drag, then escorted Myra out of the office and into the fairgrounds.

As they explored the World's Fair, most people just assumed that Ellie was a man in a costume, his movements were that natural and lifelike. The first area they explored was the Futurama plaza on the GM Pavilion, and they marveled at the vision of a future metropolis. Myra enjoyed the miniature city, but afterward, as she and Ellie looked for more diversions, she grew pensive.

"Penny for your thoughts, cutie," said her robot companion.

"Oh, I was just thinking. When time goes by, like they showed in Futurama, there's probably going to be a lot more robots, like you. Right?"

Ellie spotted an unoccupied bench and sat down. He helped the little girl climb up onto the seat beside him. "That's the idea. If there's things we can do help make peoples' lives better, then there will probably be robots around."

"Right. So I started thinking about you. And there's some stuff I don't understand."

"Well, shoot, little lady! If that's what's bothering you, just ask, and I'll tell you anything you want to know. Just fire away."

"There's two things." Myra held up a pair of fingers. "How come you talked so funny when I first met you, and now you talk more normal? And how come you smoke cigarettes?"

"Wow! You are one smart cookie! Are you sure you're only five years old?"

Myra nodded.

"Okay, here's the thing, sweetie. Those two things are related, but different, if you know what I mean."

Myra shook her head, indicating that she didn't.

"Well, take the way I talk, for instance. When the Doc first built me, all I knew how to do was say things one word at a time, and with no feeling behind them. You know, 'I… am… a… robot.' That kind of thing. But when I heard people talking, I learned how to sound more like them, like the Doc's family. He built me in his basement, can you believe it? So I learned to talk like him and his wife and his kids, because that's what I heard being spoken around me."

"So why did you talk mechanical to me before Uncle Bert told you that me and Papa were his friends?"

"Well, Doc Keeler started to worry that if people here at the Fair heard me talking like a real person, they might get scared of me." Ellie reached up and scratched his head. "Doc figures that we can gradually let me talk more normally in public, and in five or 10 years, people will be so used to me, that it won't bother them when I sound like everybody else."

Myra frowned. "But if they knew how nice you are, they wouldn't be afraid of you!"

"Thanks, cutie. But the reason you think I'm nice is because *you* are so nice. A lot of other people aren't so sweet as you, so they don't see me as being such a good guy. So like Doc says, we'll take it nice and slow."

The little girl thought about it. "I guess that makes sense. But what about the cigarettes?"

"That's kind of the other side of it. Doctor Keeler wanted to show people what kind of new technology is being used in robotics, that I can do something like inhale and exhale. But he wanted to also make it something that people are familiar with, like something just any average guy on the street might do, so he built me so that I could smoke a cigarette." Ellie looked as sheepish as a metal man possibly could look. "And the fact is, I like it. It gives me something to do so that I don't just stand around like a silly metal statue. It's a part of me, it's just how I'm made."

Myra frowned again. "I don't like smoking very much." She looked up into the robot's face and smiled. "But I guess it's okay for you."

"Thank you, ma'am!" he replied. "Any more questions?" When she shook her head no, he stood up and helped Myra to her feet. "Then let's go have some more fun!"

Before long, they found themselves at the parachute-jump ride. "Oh, Ellie! I saw this in my World's Fair funnybook!" She pulled a comic book from her little knapsack. "Papa bought this for me at the front gate. It's got stories in it with Zatara, and Gingersnap, and the Sandman, and look, here's the parachute jump!" She opened the book up to a comic strip panel featuring a man in a blue bodysuit and red cape. The setting was, in fact, the World's Fair, very nearly right where the girl and robot were standing.

Ellie opened the camera-apertures of his eyes wide, in order to take in the story. "So what is this? Who is that man in the costume?"

"That's Superman. He's got his own funnybooks, too, called 'Action.' He's from another planet, and he's extra-strong, and fast, and he helps people. See, he's catching this man who fell off the parachute ride, so he won't get killed." She turned the pages. "And here, he helped build an exhibit at the Fair for the doctors and scientists who treat babies who are sick. He's called the Man of Tomorrow, just like the Fair is about the World of Tomorrow!"

Ellie gave a low, appreciative whistle. "Whew, he really seems to be something, that's for sure. But what about the parachute jump? Your Superman book makes it look as if it might be dangerous to go on this ride."

She looked way, way up at the tower and watched as cables pulled two-person canvas seats several stories up into the air and then let them drop until a parachute deployed and allowed the participants to experience both freefall and then a cushioned landing. "Well. It's scary. But that makes it an adventure, right? Like Uncle Bert said. And you'll be there with me? Promise?"

"If you want to do it, I will be there with you. I promise."

The ride was scary. Very scary. Myra screamed for most of the way down. And then insisted that they go again. And then a third time.

———•••———

At the end of the day, they made their way back toward the electronics exhibit. Myra stopped just outside of Uncle Bert's office. "Ellie?"

"Yes, sweetie?"

"I was thinking about what you said. About robots helping people. And about how Superman helps people. And you know what?"

"What's that?"

"I think the Man of Tomorrow is a better name for *you* than for *him*. Because you're like Superman. But *you're* real. Because robots are really going to help people. And because you helped me. You helped me be brave."

Ellie scooped Myra up in his arms and hugged her.

———•••———

Myra Cohen, star graduate student of the renowned Dr. Keeler, flipped Electronico's power switch to 'on'. The familiar humming sound came from the familiar barrel chest. But his eye-apertures remained closed shut, until Myra said, "Hello, Man of Tomorrow." It was her traditional greeting to the robot, a private joke from when the two had first met some twenty years ago.

His eyes clicked open. "Hiya, kiddo!" He looked at the cigarette smoldering in Myra's hand, and asked, "Do you have one of those for me?"

Myra rolled her eyes. "Don't you think that's just a tad ironic, given the procedure we just put you through?" But she shook a cigarette out of her purse and and held the match for him as he lit it up.

"Ahhh. Ironic it may be, sweetie, but then again, I'm hardwired to be a smoker. You, on the other hand, once looked down on the habit, if my circuits don't deceive me. And they don't."

"You've got me there," Myra said with a wry grin. "Too many late nights of research and lab experiments, I'm afraid. Papa and Uncle Bert are both slave drivers. Nicotine and caffeine are the only way to make it through."

Ellie shook his head in mock sorrow. "You humans! You have the intelligence to know that cigarettes aren't good for you, but you don't have the wisdom to quit. Me, on the other hand, when all that smoke starts to gunk up my airways, then I can just have them replaced with new, clean parts. Or at least that's the theory." And now he looked intently at his friend. "How did it work out in practice?"

Myra laughed. "Aha! You were more concerned about it than you let on! Well rest assured, my fine metal chum, it worked like a charm. While you were unplugged, we put you up on the grease-rack, and your body now houses a set of brand-spanking-new fans, hoses and filters. You can smoke like a chimney, and you're still good for three years or 30,000 miles, whichever comes first!"

"Oh, that's great! Hey, let's take the new gear out for a spin! Dinner and dancing, what do you say?"

Myra paused, looked thoughtful, and then smiled. "Why not? Papa's in Washington to meet with some politicians, and Uncle Bert can get along here in the lab without me for one evening."

He took her to a nice restaurant. The robot waiters were polite and efficient. A human band played a nice mix of both old standards and new music of 1959. After dessert, and over cigarettes, they chatted about the future.

"Nothing much different for me," Ellie said, "just more of the same, acting as cheerleader for the robotics industry and helping to integrate my fellows into the human world."

"And I think my path has been determined for a couple of decades now," replied Myra. "With Papa and Uncle Bert in charge of my upbringing, I think I was destined to go into medical robotics. It's lucky for me that I love it!" she laughed.

"Well, if you are halfway as good at sticking hardware into a human body as you are at sticking it into a robot body," he thumped his own chest, "then I'd say you have quite a flair for it! Say, have you heard? There's some rumbling in the grapevine about a group of businessmen trying to mount another World's Fair out in Flushing Meadows."

"But there's already a Fair scheduled for Seattle, isn't there? The Space Needle, and all."

"Yeah, but I guess these guys loved the 1939 Fair so much, they want to try to re-create it. I can't blame them, it was some sort of wonderful, that Fair."

"Yes, it was! That's when we first met! Promise me something, will you, that we'll go to the World's Fair together again, no matter if it's in Washington state or here in New York! Or both!" She held up her glass and toasted. "To the World of the Future!"

Ellie followed suit. "To the World of the Future!"

<hr>

Ellie sat in an uncomfortable chair beside the hospital bed, watching television coverage of the Apollo 11 mission. Myra was sleeping peacefully, but the machines that kept watch on her heartbeat, pulse, and brain activity, indicated that she was coming out of her post-op slumber. Ellie closed his eye apertures in anticipation of her greeting.

"Hello, Man of Tomorrow. I could hear your chest humming from clear over here." Myra's voice was a bit groggy, but strong. The robot opened his eyes and looked down at her. "Hiya, kiddo."

He nodded toward the television set mounted on the wall. "You may want to reconsider my title, however. Maybe we should call Captain Armstrong 'the Man of Tomorrow.' He walked on the moon while you were having your beauty rest." His voice was casual, but he was watching Myra closely for any signs of discomfort or respiratory difficulties.

"Oh, phooey on Captain Armstrong. No, I take that back. Did he really walk on the moon? That's wonderful. But you're the only Man of Tomorrow that I would trust to keep an eye on the quacks they call doctors in this place while they are working on me…" She glanced down to look at herself, body hidden under sterile hospital blankets, and then looked at the monitors and computer screens that surrounded her bed. "And speaking of that… how did it go?"

Ellie smiled. "As you once said to me, 'Your body now houses a set of new fans, hoses, and filters.' Congratulations, you're the recipient of the world's first set of artificial lungs. Out with the cancer, in with the technology."

"Yes, I guess 1969 is a banner year for innovation. A man on the moon, and a machine in my chest." She looked wistful. "I wish Papa and Uncle Bert could be here to see this."

"I know. Both individually and working together, they laid the groundwork. But I know they would be just as proud of you as I am for what you've accomplished, and where you are taking their research."

"Well, I'm glad you were there to help make sure that Dr. Bloom took proper care of both my technology and my biology. Still, I would have felt safer if it had been you handling the procedure." Myra frowned. "I'm very upset that they wouldn't let me appoint *you* as the lead surgeon, and make Bloom be *your* assistant, instead of the other way around."

"I know. But I'm sure that day will be here before we know it. Humans are getting more comfortable with my kind everyday. Do you remember my friend, Lucky? Lucky LeCroix? He was one of the robots featured at the electronics display when we visited the World's Fair, the one in Queens with the Unisphere in '69."

"Oh, yes. He was nice. He was designed for some sort of piloting, wasn't he?"

"Exactly." Ellie gestured toward the television, unlit cigarette in hand. "Well, he was the co-pilot on the moonship with Armstrong. The first manned-landing on the moon had a robot as a co-pilot, you'd better believe I'm going to be milking that for all the public relations that I can!"

He reached down and pulled a bouquet of flowers out from under his chair. "And speaking of the moon, way back when I got *my* new lungs, we celebrated with a night on the town, and then watched ol' Luna rise over the water, remember?"

"I do." She smiled.

"I'd like to celebrate *your* new lungs in the same way. Would you like that?"

"I would. It's a date."

He bent down and gave her a kiss on the cheek.

• • •

"Hello, Man of Tomorrow." Myra looked up at Ellie. The characteristic hum of robot filled the room. The majority of Ellie's team were high-tech, state-of-the-art medical 'bots, with one or two highly skilled human technicians scattered among them.

"Hiya, kiddo." Roused from his meditation, the robot opened his eyes and spoke his part of the ritual, but his heart wasn't in it. Myra was far too thin, her color was bad, and she looked weak as a kitten. He tried to hide his despair from her but she knew him too well for that.

"Don't be glum, chum. Way back when we put my mechanical lungs in a decade ago, we should have realized they would outlast the rest of the body."

"Oh, but Myra." The robot sounded infinitely sad. "It's just too soon. By all rights, you should have years and years of living left from that body, that wonderful, beautiful human body."

"Yeah, but it's my own damned fault. We also should have realized that it wasn't just the lungs that were susceptible to the carcinogens in cigarettes. Like you once said, there's a difference between intelligence and wisdom." She looked over Ellie's shoulder at his team. of technicians. "Oh, well. It gives me the chance to make another contribution to science, I suppose."

"I suppose."

Myra gestured feebly for him to lean down toward her. "It's scary. But it's an adventure, right? And you'll be here with me?" she whispered. Ellie could so clearly see in her little girl he had met at the 1939 World's Fair, the little girl who had chosen a robot over Superman, because the robot was real.

"I will. I'll be here with you. I promise. Sweet dreams, sweetheart." His kissed her cheek, and then motioned for the robot behind him to begin the anesthesia.

Myra heard the hum that she had associated with robots for nearly half a century. And more than that, she felt it, she *felt* that old, familiar, lovable hum. But she wouldn't look, not yet. Not until she heard his voice.

"Hello, Woman of Tomorrow."

"Hiya, kiddo," she replied, opening her eye-apertures to see Ellie smiling down at her.

One day in 1939, Myra began her journey toward the future. Forty years later, she arrived.

Some characters are crafted, others discovered by their authors. In this editor's opinion, characters of the latter category ring truest. In our next story, Ms Morrone peers back into the boyhood of such a character, so that she can better understand his origin.

This story itself has an unusual genesis, she tells us. It was born decades back while battling a near-fatal illness, forgotten for years, with no memory of having written it.

The King's Contest

By Wenda Morrone

"Majesty, I regret to disturb you," First Minister Greaves said.

Majesty: the word they used publically for a matter of urgency.

The king's frown was as startled as it was severe. He had been a soldier, and a fine one before he had been chosen king. One of his few absolutes was, that time he spent with old comrades was not to be interrupted. Greaves gave these comrades a fleeting sideways glance to suggest privacy.

The king's frown deepened. "I have no secrets from these men."

So be it. "Boys have broken into the caves."

The king rose at once and came away, not bothering to excuse himself. "They have been brought to the Hall of Martyrs?"

"Yes, Sire. One is even now in extremis."

"We go at once."

The king strode to the carport. Greaves trotted to keep up.

Years earlier on Academy Planet the king had been Greaves' student. But once chosen king, he was compelled to live in King's Time, while Greaves had spent decades over his lifetime locked in genesis. Now he was by many years the younger man. But the king had the lean body of the soldier he had been. Greaves was only as fit as rules required him to be, his eyes deeply lined by a scholar's hours bent over a reading screen. Of course he had to trot to keep up.

Once in the aircar and whining toward the museum that housed the Hall of Martyrs, the king said, "It was my understanding, First Minister, that the cave entrance had been terraformed in the same way—with the same intended permanence—we shape planets to our needs. If it has broken down, the Colony Planets are endangered as well."

"The entrance remains pristine, Sire. A boy found a different way in. He showed others."

Often the former soldier seemed impatient at the limitations of a king. "Surely in a thousand years a way could have been found to put the caves beyond the reach of boys forever."

"I concur, Sire."

If the caves had ever had another name, it was lost—part of the shunning centuries before, perhaps, when radioactive detritus had been sealed in barrels, sealed again in caves deep in mountains of what had once been known as Nevada. So said the archives. Some said the barrels must lie undisturbed for a thousand years, others said ten thousand.

The planners were all former boys. How could they have chosen so poorly? Boys broke into the caves a mere sixty years later. They, their families, and many who came in contact, died.

Their deaths were well-publicized. A web of wires, razor-sharp, charged with the power of that time, was added to the caves' new seal. It was sixty-some years before boys broke in again. Thus began an unfortunate pattern: men contrived safety devices, boys outwitted them in sixty-some years.

"How old are the boys?" asked the king. "How many?"

"The ringleader claims to be fourteen. The others are ten, eleven. Seven boys altogether."

"Any highborn?"

Highborn were far too well watched. Greaves did not say so. "Sons of citizens only."

"So is it always. And of them, how many clones?"

"Three that we know of."

The aircar hovered for the king and First Minister to alight on the street of the museum. A step behind the king, Greaves mounted the stairs. They were marble, hollowed by centuries of use. Greaves tried to picture the many footsteps it had taken to wear away the stone. He looked at old paintings of crowded streets and marketplaces with equal fascination.

Today, imagery allowed distant viewers to examine pictures from every angle, thus the museum served the planet. But distant viewers were few.

Once past the line of guards, Greaves paused. The king looked back. "Well?"

"I see no the decontamination chamber, Sire."

"Unnecessary. Radiation poisoning isn't contagious."

He would have continued. Greaves found he could not.

The king was never openly condescending, but he could be exceedingly courteous. "You believe myth rather than our Tech Minister's analyses, First Minister?"

"I read his reports, Sire," Greaves said woodenly. "But I am a historian by training. Our women are unfruitful, our numbers dwindle, across all castes. The archives tell me our losses began after the waste was sealed in the caves. When the caves were breeched sixty years ago, nearly fifty died. Fifty souls meant less to them then than seven mean to us today."

"Women fail to breed as well in the Colony Planets, First Minister."

All settlements who had migrated from King's Earth. Greaves did not say so. It could be unwise to know better than the king. He ordered his feet to step forward. For a wonder, they obeyed.

The museum's halls save one were empty. Their footsteps echoed, it seemed to Greaves, all the way from the lobby to the third floor gallery where the boys and their parents were housed. It was said this was done to allow parents to stay with their sons until their deaths. In fact, guards at all possible exits made the stay mandatory. The boys' clothing had been destroyed, the boys themselves scrubbed and decontaminated immediately upon discovery, long before they reached the Hall of Martyrs. So it was said. So it was always said, but on the last occasion, besides the packs of boys who had played—played!—in the caves and sickened and died, a parent had also.

The smell of medicines and cleansing ionizers grew stronger as they neared the gallery. At the doorway, a doctor said in the hushed, affronted voice with which doctors confronted death, "One boy has already reached the final stage."

"Yes, the First Minister has told me."

The king might have begun as a soldier, but his touch with people was masterly. He went immediately to the boy. Easy to discern him— he looked scorched from the inside out, eyes glassy, lungs trembling like a bird's with the struggle to breathe.

Greaves waved all but the boy's parents to a distance. He cast a surreptitious glance at lenses in the walls. He had directed the Media Minister to activate them, though he hadn't expected so useful an opportunity so early.

Other parents looked at the dying boy, away, then unwillingly back, as if they saw their own sons, Greaves thought. And rightly: all but one already displayed heavy burns. Two others were flushed as well, hair damp with sweat. The seventh had hair redder than any possible flush. His bed was set at a distance from the others, perhaps because he was older—clearly the fourteen-year-old in the report. Or perhaps, because he had no family present. Instead he strummed a battered instrument. His movements looked practiced, though the results were untuneful.

Childhood superstition lingered: Greaves had to force himself to approach the redheaded boy. Once near, he could see a single burn along his collarbone. Sweat beaded his hairline.

"You're Angus Mackenzie?"

"Who's asking?"

"First Minister Greaves." He asked again, "You're the boy Mackenzie?"

"Plain Angus, thanks. I haven't made my mind up about Mackenzie."

"When do your parents arrive?"

"We won't talk about my ma."

Greaves nodded as if Angus' belligerence were remarkable. He waved at the instrument. "You found the guitar here?"

"It's mine. A man I knew gave it to me. And it isn't a guitar, it's a samisen."

White-knuckled fist on its neck. Lips drawn back from his teeth, not a smile. His skin was nearly as gray-white as his teeth.

"He taught you to play?" Greaves kept his voice mild.

Angus resumed his strumming. "Only I broke a string a few months back. That's why it sounds lame. I have to keep reworking the fingering."

"Tell me what you need. I'll procure it."

He didn't know why he promised—there was little music to Angus' playing. Perhaps because the boy was dying. Perhaps because he behaved as if dying didn't matter.

The strumming abruptly took on a pattern and a volume. Angus' voice rose.

"I dream of apples and wake to dying.

When I get closer, will I hear dead birds sing?"

His voice was nearer a man's than a boy's, but high, with an unexpected sweetness. It carried throughout the gallery. Parents drew breaths like hisses of pain. The boys looked gratified, even soothed. The king turned to listen.

Greaves found it difficult to say calmly, "Go on."

"That's all I have so far. It's for the contest."

"You—you know of the contest? Who told you?" Of all the rules, surely this was the most stringent: boys were never to know how public their dying was to be, or why.

Angus looked at Greaves as though he were the child. "Everybody knows. How do you think we knew we were doing something dangerous?" His eyes still glistened at the thought.

Reckless, not ill-informed. Greaves found it difficult to make himself believe it.

"Besides," said the boy, "what else have we got to talk about except the contest? Or think about?"

"You plan to enter?"

"Why shouldn't I?"

Greaves strove to look unaffected. He knew he failed.

"Do I know I'll be dead when the king picks a winner?" Angus spoke Greaves' thought for him. "I don't think so. Suppose I am? No worries. You put the word out I won, Ma will turn up for the prize money."

Greaves suspected his belligerence hid fear. Surely.

"Did you stay behind, perhaps, while the others explored?" he asked. "That's why their illness is so much more advanced?"

Belligerence turned to scorn. "Who said that? I'm the one who found the way in. I been there on my own lots of times before I agreed to take them. Ol' Reg is dying so soon because he's a clone."

"What makes you think so? Because he resembles his father?"

Deeper scorn. "When you're dying, you look like somebody who's dying. Those other two—" A jerk of his head. "They're clones, too. They'll be next."

It didn't take great insight to see who would be next. But then the pale pitiless gaze turned to Greaves.

"You're a clone, too, aren't you?"

Greaves had to keep himself from making a fear sign. He could only ask a second time, "What makes you think so?"

"It's like your edges are blurry. You're not as wavery as some," he said as if to be reassuring. "Like maybe you're a one or a two. I bet Reg is a five. But you're a watcher like them."

"A watcher?" Greaves repeated.

"Other people do things, you watch and tell about them. I'm right, aren't I?"

An insight that came with the nearness of Angus' own death? Greaves said stiffly, "I am a historian."

"Like I said. What did your dad do?"

"Also a historian." A more significant one. When people spoke of Greaves' books, it was Greaves' father they meant. Perhaps his edges had not been so wavery.

Angus looked over at the sickest boy, the one he called Reg. Greaves followed Angus's gaze just as the boy laid his twig of a hand in the king's and died. The king bowed his head. He smoothed the eyes shut, then stood and held the mother as her wails rose to screams.

While the world watched.

Greaves left Angus and approached the king. "Majesty—"

The king excused himself as soon as was reasonable. Greaves led him to a corner sheltered from the lenses, where he could speak and the king could hear without being observed. He repeated what Angus had said.

"Angus has been in the caves most often and he is the least affected?" asked the king.

"So he claims. He would tell you more, I think. I'm a clone. He thinks poorly of us."

"Then he thinks wrongly. Clones have a strength whole men lack. Detachment comes more easily to you."

Detachment. Watching. Historian. Different names for the same attribute, an attribute of men who were not whole. The thought was unpleasing.

The king looked at the redheaded boy. He was talking to an attendant, pointing above his bed at an immense oil painting where trout leapt out of the water and turned into bowties. He appeared to be asking for darts.

"Target practice would be an excellent use for that painting," the king said. "Very well, I'll see what he'll tell me."

Greaves trailed him discreetly.

As the king approached, Angus matter-of-factly made room on the bed for him to sit. "You talking to me because you think I'm next? Because I'm not."

"Sire," Greaves prompted under his breath. Both ignored him.

"This little burn? I've had lots of them. Give it a week, it'll be gone."

"You're doing better than the others," the king agreed. "They're too weak to tell me what happened. Perhaps you can."

"You mean, how we got in? There was a rockslide. When I started poking around, I found a back way in. I didn't even know it was, you know, those caves until I saw the barrels."

"Your entrance will be terraformed. What did you find?"

Angus eyed the king before he spoke. "I only looked at the nearest ones."

On the other side of the bed, Greaves pressed his hands hard together. Perhaps it could keep him from showing his fear. Help him focus as a historian. Assess what the boy said as mere information.

The king—the soldier—showed only mild curiosity. "Then tell me of those."

Angus sent his gaze around as if for eavesdroppers. He stopped to scowl at the trout painting.

"I will order darts to be provided to you," the king said. "The drums?"

Angus lowered his voice. "They were on their sides. Not rolling on account of it's, you know, a cave."

"The surface would be too uneven. Yes, I see. I'm not here to judge you, Angus. Did you tip the drums over?"

He shook his red hair till it flew. "Maybe the bulging did it. Because they're leaking."

"Leaking?"

"Oily stuff."

Greaves wondered if fear alone could stop a human heart. If a clone's heart was more susceptible.

Still the king sounded merely curious. "You deduced that from the way it looked? Or you touched it?"

"Think I'm crazy? I stirred it with a stick. It's thick. It makes little rainbows if you shine a laserlight."

"How many drums leak?"

Angus shrugged. "I only saw the ones in front. Ol' Reg and the others got scared and bolted. They didn't know the way out. I had to show them."

"I don't blame them for their fear," said the king.

The boy's look was scornful. "Doc says people will keep dying for nine thousand more years. You believe that?" At least this time the boy added, "Sire?"

"So I am told."

Angus's defiance went with his hair. "I'm fine. I always look pale. Everybody from around the caves does."

"May your health continue."

The king rose and gestured to Greaves to come away. He said, "Get him the darts. Also a different instrument."

"He calls it a samisen," Greaves said. "A gift from someone."

"He is correct. It was a played by Japanese courtesans a thousand years ago. More. His benefactor mocked him." Greaves must have looked startled. The king said almost bitterly, "I was more than a soldier before I became a king, First Minister."

As was any man, even a clone who became First Minister. "Clearly, Sire."

"Find an instrument that both sounds and looks beautiful," said the king. "This is a museum, after all. Let us put at least one of its objects to use for this little while."

"It will be done."

The king strode out of the Hall of Martyrs with a crisp salute to the guards. Greaves trotted after.

The king paused on the stairs. "Could the boy be lying about the drums, Greaves?"

"Boys brag about stupid things, Sire."

"And do them, too. But if he was that close to the contaminants and were to survive—"

Survive: live to pass on the death within him. Clones would suffer first and most, Greaves believed Angus about that.

"Is it your wish that the boy be studied, Sire? If researchers could find why he remains healthy when his fellows have been struck down—isolate something in his blood—"

The king gave him a sidewise glance. "I suppose it must be done."

"If you wish me to order otherwise—"

The king's gaze was fierce. "Can you, First Minister?" He waved up the stairs toward the gallery where the boys lay. "You are a historian. Can your archives show you a better way to bring an end to that?"

"I will speak with the Science Minister."

In the aircar, Greaves said, "The boy Angus means to enter the contest."

"That is obscene," said the king.

"He thinks differently, Sire. He has not the same boundaries."

The king stared at something only he saw. "I knew soldiers who appeared genuinely fearless. Never a good choice to lead, but by the gods they could accomplish amazing things. I always wondered if they lived in a different world from mine. If things that alarmed me—terrified me—were simply part of the landscape to them."

"And was it so, Sire?"

"None lived long enough to ask." He turned to Greaves. "Review the contest with me, First Minister."

The contests had begun a few hundred years earlier. The King's Council of that era reasoned that as well as improved defenses for the caves, a sufficiently appalled citizenry might better restrain boys from breaking in. At the inevitable next incident, a contest was announced to select the most effective warning for the future. Thus each boy's illness and death could be publicized at every stage as an excuse to inspire entries to the contest. Competition gave many more opportunities to stress the horrors. The years between break-ins did not increase, but by the time that had been determined, the contests had become tradition. Towns participated separately, sending winning entries to cities, and so on, until the final presentations represented all continents.

On the screen before him, the king traced the first warning sign from a thousand years earlier, three black diamonds leapt out of a glaring yellow triangle with DANGER printed underneath.

"How could that have frightened a boy away? Any boy?"

"Clearly it did not."

Over the centuries there had been paintings by children, plays, clothing designs. The one thing they had in common was increasingly detailed coverage of the victims' dying. A post-mortem picture had actually won the last contest. Shirts and gowns printed with it were still available for purchase.

The king averted his eyes from it.

"The purpose of the contest is to warn, Sire," Greaves said.

"You mean to horrify. Make boys afraid until their boyhood has passed, perhaps even to pass the fear to their child. Yet these boys must have passed postings with this very picture to reach the caves."

"Perhaps the boy Angus found a way that avoided them."

"Or perhaps not. Sooner or later, a soldier must learn to live with fear. This boy may already have mastered it. Sometimes it's a useful skill. Not always." The king sighed. "Put forward announcements of the contest, First Minister. You will notify me when I must visit again?"

"As you wish."

"Interrupt me when necessary."

The easiest of the king's commands to fill was the purchase of darts. Within minutes of Greaves' delivery, Angus had the boys divided into teams and the Hall of Martyrs echoed with challenges and threats. And laughter. When their energy flagged—too soon, far too soon, particularly for the two boys who were clones—Angus challenged Greaves.

Greaves looked at the darts. All the boys had handled them, many times. He managed to suppress his shudder and shook his head. "You and I have another task. The king has promised you the use of any instrument in the museum."

"You have one like mine?"

"The king feels when you know the history of the samisen you will choose otherwise."

He repeated the king's words. Angus' response fascinated and chilled him: deepening anger at having been made fun of, clearly, yet how did he convey it? He seemed neither more flushed nor paler than he already was—perhaps his skin could not change—but his intensity built until it was poised like a blow.

"The museum has many choices," Greaves added hastily before he became the target.

Angus bounced to his feet. "Great. Where?"

"My dear child, you can't leave the Hall of Martyrs." He spoke still faster as Angus seemed to coil even deeper within himself. "But the imagery is readily available."

Greaves reached beyond Angus, taking care to stay more than an arm's length, and pressed one of the sensors. An instrument appeared on the screen, revolved to show every side, faded. Another appeared.

"Choose whatever you like," said Greaves. "It will be brought to you."

"If I decide I don't like it, I choose again," Angus said.

Could decontamination rays damage an instrument? Greaves had no doubt what the king would say. He need not know.

He nodded.

The problem didn't arise. Angus fixed on something called a mandolin: round-bellied, a rich red-brown wood inset with flowers and vines of other woods. Already centuries old. Far too beautiful for this street boy. Greaves waved to an attendant to fetch it.

"Plus books on how to play it," Angus said. "I'm not wasting time blundering around."

Perhaps the boy understood how little remained to him after all.

By the following day Angus already seemed able to accompany his songs. The mandolin's sound was rich and full, not harsh. Perhaps it resembled the samisen more closely than Greaves realized. By the time the king paid his fourth sad visit, Angus played a dirge with a skill that would have impressed anyone.

By then the painting above Angus' bed was pockmarked beyond recognition.

Greaves watched the king take note of both without comment.

Instead he said to Angus, "How does your song for the contest progress?"

Angus gripped the neck of the mandolin like a live thing, teeth bared. "You'll hear it when it's ready."

"Sire," Greaves prompted under his breath. Once again both ignored him. The king merely nodded and left, Greaves a few steps behind. He could still hear Angus behind him, strumming. The mellow sound followed them past the guards and down the stairs.

Angus had protected his other poor instrument passionately, too. Odd for music to matter to such a boy. Odder still that he should prove gifted.

Time—past time—that Angus be moved to the Hall of Science, where his inexplicable health could be investigated.

The night before Angus was to be transferred, Greaves broke into the king's chambers and actually shook his sovereign by the shoulder.

"Forgive me, Majesty! You told me to interrupt you at any time."

The king shook off sleep. "And meant it. Another boy is dying?"

"Much worse. Sire, the boy Angus has escaped."

"Who brings you this news, Greaves?"

"My camera is focused on them always. I can see his empty bed. The nearest window is open. A rope is looped around its center molding."

"Primitive but effective. You went to the Hall of Martyrs today. Was there anything that might have triggered this?"

Why did the king waste time with questions when this boy could even now be spreading his plague? But the king was the king.

"Angus sang us the first two verses of his song," said Greaves. "There was some talk. He's—he was to be transferred to the Ministry of Technology this very morning. The two remaining boys were upset, they felt abandoned."

The king shrugged on a heavy robe and strode from the room.

Greaves scrambled to follow. "I have alerted the guards, Sire—"

"I don't doubt it."

An aircar whined them to the Hall of Martyrs. The king took the outside steps in threes with Greaves panting behind. At the massive front doors, guards in gloves and gas masks held a squirming boy in their heavily gloved hands. His red hair lit up the dark. The priceless mandolin lay at his feet.

Greaves sighed with relief. "So, Angus—" he began.

"Release him," the king said to the guards. "Leave us. And rid yourself of those absurd costumes."

The guards obeyed with alacrity, backing out of hearing, but not sight. The gloves and masks remained.

Angus stuck out his chin. "Another ten minutes, I'd have been gone."

"That was my hope, certainly," said the king.

Greaves smothered an explanation, but it wouldn't have mattered. Neither noticed him.

Angus said, "Liar!"

To the king.

Before Greaves could force himself to clout the boy, the king said, "I was once a soldier, Angus. I have old comrades with useful skills. How often do you imagine coils of rope can be found ready to hand by your window? Your oddly unlocked window?"

Greaves headed off further insolence by asking, "You knew of Angus' transfer before I told you, Sire?"

"You know well, First Minister, everyone here is on someone's secret payroll. Occasionally even mine."

He turned to the boy. "If you leave here, Angus—"

"When."

"Very well, when you leave, one of three things will happen. The most likely is that people will learn of your escape, hunt you down, and tear you apart like a pack of dogs. Many people still believe radiation poisoning is contagious."

"More likely they'll touch me for luck," said the boy. "And number two?"

The king sighed. "You will die alone, in pain and in fear, instead of amongst people who would try to ease your going."

Briefly, Angus's eyes reflected the horror of deaths so recently witnessed. Then he glowered. "You mean people working me over in a lab like an animal."

Greaves smothered an exclamation. Angus transferred his glower. "Your idea, right? Why? You're supposed to be a watcher, not a doer."

Greaves was taken aback. More: defensive. "If you are immune to radiation, Angus, and the reason could be discovered, others might be helped to develop the same immunity."

"Who? Mutts like me who live near the caves?"

Greaves said stiffly, "Naturally."

Angus' grin seemed menacing. "You mean, after all you clones are safe. If you ever are."

He turned to the king. "You said three things. What's the third?" Then, reluctantly, "Sire?"

"You may survive," said the king. "You would be the first known to do so."

"That's what he's afraid of, isn't it?" He jerked his head toward Greaves. "That's why they're taking me away. If they can't make some kind of cure out of me, at least they can keep me locked me up like a freak. Is that what you want, too? Sire?"

"The part of me that is merely a man does. By far the largest part."

"Then why help me? If you're not lying."

The king stared out at the empty street, perhaps imagining it as crowded as historians said it had once been. "The part of me that is king compels me to say to you, Go. Grow to manhood. Father children who grow in turn. Live."

The boy's eyes shifted. Without warning he seized the mandolin and bolted.

Greaves grabbed for him. The— king knocked his outstretched arms aside. Angus dodged out down the stairs into the dark.

Guards ran forward. The king waved them back.

Greaves stared at the ground, ashamed. How could he have so misunderstood the king's intent for the boy?

Still, he owed his sovereign honesty.

"Workers here will tell their secret employers of this escape, Sire," Greaves said. "Rumors will spread. You spoke truly. Angus will be set upon and killed. When the Media Minister hears of it, his death may even become publicity for the contest."

"My comrades will try to watch over him until fresh disasters capture the public's attention."

"Sire, you are the king," Greaves said. "You are free to make any decision you choose and let me find out with others. Why do you share this with me now?"

The king looked out into the dark as if he could still see the fleeing boy. More to himself than to Greaves he said, "Can we frighten ourselves successfully for another nine thousand years? Will enough of us live to do so? But if this boy survives… If he breeds…"

Greaves dug his fingers into his palms and breathed deep. "Your First Minister exists only to serve, Majesty. My views appear to be inappropriate. Someone else might serve you better."

The king turned his gaze from the street to Greaves. He seemed to look from a long distance. He clasped Greaves' shoulder and said, as if his words had to cross that distance, "You mean we have burdened you with our service too long, old friend. Time and past time you returned to Academy Planet. Who better than you to write the history of our future?"

Two decades locked in genesis merely to reach Academy Planet. The king was right: by the time Greaves awoke, the story of this incident—of this contest—of Angus—would be over. However it ended, Greaves would write as historian, not participant. A watcher, according to the boy. A historian's detachment, according to the king.

Greaves bowed his head. "I pray the decisions you must make will be easier when you are served by strangers, Majesty."

"I share your prayer."

From the street below the boy's voice came back to them, singing the last verse of the song that would go on to win the king's contest, though an unknown sang it — perhaps Angus feared he would be imprisoned if he surfaced so soon. The ballad was still famous when Greaves reached Academy Planet two decades later. Apparently Angus felt safe enough by then to reveal that he had grown to manhood and added the name StarDrifter. People embraced all his songs as they had the first. But none ever unsettled Greaves like that one, Angus' high, eerily sweet voice echoing back down the dark street toward Greaves and the king as if from the very cave that should have killed him:

Death whispers behind my shoulder,

telling me I'm past due

to find out how much dying I can live with.

How much can you?

Throughout his career Mr. Bruner has been a communicator, turning out scripts, articles, and more. Of late he has been writing stories in his favorite genre, citing Andre Norton, Robert Heinlein, and Arthur C. Clarke as significant influences.

Rockets ships plying interstellar space have long been a staple of science fiction, perhaps because they harken back to an age when crossing an ocean took days and weeks, and were sometimes fraught with peril. These vast, space-faring liners are open to infinite story possibilities, a comforting thought to any science fiction writer, and we hope readers feel the same.

Deadman's Hand

By Rick Bruner

I was one of the newly hatched. The old was giving way to the new. It used to be if you wanted a pilot's berth with one of the companies it meant grinding your way through one of the military academies and spending eight or ten years in uniform before you could hope to even be considered for a job.

But the companies were out to make a profit, and overpaying for astrogators and junior pilots irked them to no end. So, in 2414 they managed to ram a special bill through the Combined Space Authority allowing them to establish their own training schools and thereby ending the United Earth Space Service's monopoly on pilots and lowering wages at the same time.

It was good business on their part and appealed to me in that I could skip the years of spit and polish and military ass kissing that was enough to make apprenticing as a plumber attractive. Now just four years at a company school and you were ready to see the worlds. I graduated in the first class.

My first berth was on the old Alhambra, a passenger-freighter on the Cappella B route. The 'Ham was a venerable old space harlot. Alhambra wasn't even her original name. She had been christened the North Star back in 2172, back before ion drive. She'd plied the long freefall run from Earth to the Mars colonies.

Later, after they ripped out her chemical rocket engines and installed a reactor, she became the Einstein, one of the first torch ships, with their ability to maintain a constant boost they brought the entire solar system within easy reach. Finally, in 2203, she was refitted with the Misian-Jorgenson projectors and now used the light pressure from the sun itself to turn voyages of months into weeks or even days.

She was a big roomy vessel, which suited both the company and the passengers. The staterooms were spacious and there was an abundance of cargo space. She wasn't top of the line, but she was a comfortable old girl who knew her way around. For me, she was my first ship and I was in love.

This was fortunate, since I quickly discovered I was not very popular with my crewmates. There is a drawback at being a "first" that I had never considered. I joined the 'Ham as the only member of the control room gang who was not a veteran of the military space services. Under a good captain this sort of situation could be handled. Unfortunately, while Captain Reynolds knew how to plot courses and compute parking orbits, he was somewhat oblivious to crew dynamics.

It was hard to really blame him. The 'Ham carried a crew of almost 300; most of them cooks, stewards, waiters, bartenders and whatever else was needed to cater to 1,200 paying passengers. The old lady, in that regard, was remarkably like the grand ocean going ships that had plied the earth's seas in the late nineteenth and early twentieth centuries.

The crew fell under the command of the First Officer. Mr. Taylor was also former military, but his billet had been as adjutant to the commander of Henshaw Field, Marsbase. According to the org charts, he was responsible for the crew, but as long as Mr. Hollister, the purser, kept his side of the ship's operations in order, Mr. Taylor didn't interfere. Likewise, Commander Nelson ran his engineering section. In theory and in practice, this takes the load off the captain so he can worry about the control room and getting everyone from point A to point B. Taylor made sure the passengers were comfortable and Captain Reynolds drove the bus.

Reynolds had been in space for a long time. As was his prerogative, he was not a watch standing officer, so the day to day administration of the control room fell to the watch duty officers, in my case, Mr. Jeffery Wittimore, Major UESS retired. I had issues with the retired part, Witty acted like he'd never mustered out. If an ashtray needed emptying, he made sure I was the one to empty it. If the gang needed coffee, I got to serve it. I was shown the polishing clothes and made familiar with every bit of exposed metal on the control deck. He seemed determined to make me atone for the years of service I had managed to avoid.

I set my teeth and grimly handled each little job, figuring that as the trip wore on he'd get bored and ease up. I was mistaken; he had a remarkable tenacity for getting under one's skin. But if he hoped I would quit, or that my attention to my other duties would slack, he was mistaken. I was resolved to wait him out.

Socially I was a pariah. There were the military protocols and in addition, no one wanted to incur Witty's wrath. So I messed alone, watched the videos alone; it was shaping up as a very lonely trip.

As even my entry into the exercise room killed conversation and elicited calculated snubs, I began to avoid the gymnasium in favor of walking the decks. I always went below K deck, the last of the passenger decks, into the service areas to avoid contact with any of the bridge gang. To the rest of the crew I was just another one of the ship's officers, to be avoided if possible.

It was on one of these daily walks as I passed an open compartment door that I heard the sound of cards being shuffled. Peeking in,

I saw four men seated around a table. One of them noticed me and prodded the others. The dealer looked up and spoke.

"You play poker, bud?"

I nodded, trying and failing to place their faces.

"I mean real poker; Five card draw, stud, none of this hold 'em crap?"

"I play poker," I laughed, "and none of that hold 'em crap."

"Then have a seat my friend," he replied. "Dolan's the name. That's Cohan, Ebberly and Newcomb. Quarter ante, two dollar limit on raises and the game is five card draw."

"Thanks," I eased into an empty chair nodding to the others "Name's Wilkerson."

"Well, Wilkerson, I hope you have lots of cash. I need to build up my fund for next planetside leave."

"Don't let him rattle you kid," warned Ebberly. "If he played as good a game as he talked he'd own this bucket by now."

"By the way, in here we don't talk shop, and there is no rank," explained Cohan. "We are just here to play poker."

I heaved a sigh. It was nice to just be part of something. I hadn't realized how lonely I had grown in the five weeks in the 'Ham. The banter and gentle insults were like a balm for my battered psyche. I had found someone who treated me like one of them, not an outsider who needed to be thumped constantly.

Money changed hands, but no one was a big winner or loser. The final hand came down to Dolan and me, the money in the pot would just about bring me even for the night. I called his raise and laid down my hand, Queens and fours, two pair.

"Read 'em and weep kid," Dolan said smiling as he laid down a pair of aces and two eights, all black. "Just one more successful evening for old Papa Dolan."

"Imagine that," said Cohen, "the Dead Man's Hand."

Dolan laughed. "Well it's a good thing I'm not superstitious."

"The Dead Man's hand?" I asked, feeling silly.

"Ancient history, earthside kid," explained Ebberly. "Supposedly it was the hand Wild Bill Hickok was holding when he got shot in Deadwood."

"Cohen compensates for his lack in figuring percentages by having lots of useless facts at hand,' laughed Newcomb.

"Not a bad night, kid," said Dolan, as the game broke up. "You know how to play poker."

"Yeah," I replied. "I played well enough to help your leave fund. Hopefully I will have the chance to win some of it back next time. You always play here?"

Dolan looked me up and down then laughed. "Yeah, kid, every Thursday night. As for getting your money back, well I certainly hope not."

I glanced at the compartment number as I left M41.

For the next few days, Witty ran me ragged, as he was able to find annoying little tasks that extended my day well beyond my normal watch. I didn't mind much though; the poker game and the camaraderie of Dolan, Cohan, Ebberly and Newcomb had refreshed my spirit. I was looking forward to another chance to play, even if I didn't recoup my losses.

Four days later I was back on M deck. I walked the entire deck three times but compartment M41 was nowhere to be found. I managed to snag a steward who wasn't quick enough to avoid me and asked him.

"Where is compartment M41?"

"Sorry sir," he replied. "There is no compartment 41 on this deck."

He escaped while I pondered his answer. I decided I must have read the number wrong so I made quick searches on N and L decks.

Neither held the compartment I was looking for. Puzzled, I made my way back to quarters.

"This is crazy!" I thought. "I must have gotten turned around somehow. Tomorrow I will go the First Officer to see if I can find Dolan or one of the others and get directions to the game."

"Dolan, no I have no Dolan's on my crew roster," the First Officer's clerk looked at me quizzically. "Sorry sir."

"Well how about Ebberly or Cohan or Newcomb?" I responded. "Maybe Dolan was a nickname."

"No, none of those names match either." The clerk closed his roster screen. "You sure they were maintenance and housekeeping rather than control room or engineering?"

"No, I'm not sure. I will check with engineering… maybe someone there knows who they are. Thanks."

"No problem Mr. Wilkerson, have a good one."

I was scheduled to be on watch so I made my way to the bridge. I was still mumbling and distracted enough that I managed to bump into Witty as I entered.

"Watch it Wilkerson! Keep your mind on what you're supposed to be about!"

"Yes sir," I replied hastily.

"And what were you muttering?'

"Oh nothing sir," I evaded. "Just a personal matter."

"Out with it, Mr. Wilkerson." Witty moved to block my path. "There are no personal matters on this bridge. You should know that what we do here is too important to allow anyone to be distracted by petty little matters."

"Yes sir," I looked at him. "In fact, maybe you can help; I was trying to locate a couple of crewmen I met recently. They aren't on the Purser's roster so perhaps they are in engineering. The names are Dolan, Cohan, Ebberly and Newcomb. Do you know them?"

Witty suddenly blanched. "Are you trying to be funny, Mr. Wilkerson?"

"What? No not at all, sir." I replied. "I met them a few days ago. We played poker. I went back last night hoping to find the game again but it seems I misread the compartment number and couldn't find it."

"And what compartment were you looking for, Mister Wilkerson?"

"M41." I said. "At least that is what I remember, sir."

"'This ship hasn't had a compartment with that designation for over 100 years, Mr. Wilkerson. Now who has put you up to this? Tell me right now!"

I squared my shoulders and looked him in the eye. "No one put me up to anything sir. If you can't help me then say so. I mean no disrespect, but all I asked was a simple question."

Witty looked at me for a long moment, and then turned. "Follow me, Wilkerson."

I shrugged and followed him to his control station. He tapped a few keys and then looked up at me. "Maybe you got the names wrong. Look at these faces and tell me if you see the men you are talking about."

I moved around the desk and looked at the display. Cohen was in the first row, Dolan in the next row and Ebberly was three pages further in. Newcomb I found last. I pointed them all out to him.

"Those are the men." I stated firmly. "I am positive."

Witty drew a deep breath. "You may have been the butt of an elaborate practical joke, Wilkerson, I don't know, but at least you picked out the right men; Dolan, Cohan, Ebberly and Newcomb are all dead."

He raised his hand to stifle my protest. "They have been dead for over 100 years. They were playing cards in compartment 41. There was a blowout on M deck. Back then this ship hauled freight and only carried a crew of about 25. They were trapped there and breach was serious. The repair crews were unable to reach them before the compartment air gave out. The intercom was still working and according to the log, they joked and played cards until the end. When they refitted the ship that compartment was eliminated."

"But sir," I protested. "These men were real. We talked and laughed. It was a good time."

"I understand, Wilkerson and I will look into the matter," his tone softer. "Obviously, someone is up to no good, and I will see if I can get to the bottom of it."

"Yes, sir," I mumbled, in my confusion and turned away.

"By the way Wilkerson," Witty said very softly. "How much did you contribute to Dolan's leave fund?"

The rites and rituals of death are forever with us, despite advances in medicine and pharmacology. Accompanying them while standing discretely in the background, are everyday practitioners of the business of death. In every era, past, present, and in this story—the future, every mortal generation faces the ancient question: what do we do with our dead?

Thresher Gray is pursuing a graduate degree in Chicago.

Drift

By Thresher Grey

Emmit hadn't made a decision yet. The curator had been lurking determinedly since the memorial began, hoping to extract an answer. Emmit glanced in his direction, and the tiny chap pretended to readjust a vase. The man had a perpetual and unnatural cheeriness about him, but had been running the remembrance hall for at least six centuries, and resignation had long since settled into every crease on his face. Emmit wouldn't be able to evade him for much longer.

He veered to the left and wandered down an empty hallway. The last guests were trickling out at this point. Emmit knew that his brother Berstwnn would be posted near the hall entrance, waiting to accept a final round of sympathetic handshakes, nodding stoically at each departee. Emmit and Berstwnn didn't speak much. Emmit blamed the age difference; Berstwnn's children were almost twice Emmit's age.

He also blamed Berstwnn's personality. It resembled generic brand laundry detergent—boring yet abrasive. Their mother had apparently agreed. Her will had left Emmit, not the eldest, in charge of the post-mortem aspect of her life. Berstwnn had accordingly acted very put-upon all week.

"Can you distribute the programs? I would do it myself, but… well probably just better to let you handle it."

This was in addition to the usual slew of patronizing remarks about school, women, the weather—whatever problems Emmit could possibly be causing the family. Emmit, having reached an empty room, plopped down on a fat little divan. He massaged away the headache building behind his temples and thought about tissue digestion.

Illness had come upon their mother quickly. A sudden fever, a symptom of some emergent infection, sent her to the treatment center for a standard microinjection. But she withered anyway. It happened. Even in this day and age, even to a person as young as his mother. A woman with dark hair and golden eyes, she laughed at everything, and smelled clean—like clear water and baby powder. By the time Emmit got to the hospital she was dead. The doctor practically shook with nerves as she apprised him. Emmit got the idea that she had never given bad news to someone who hadn't been expecting it before. With a referral to the remembrance hall and an awkward shoulder pat, Emmit was left to take care of the arrangements.

He had two decisions to make. The first was how to handle the body. Obviously, there was cremation. Not very ecologically friendly, but it was still traditional enough to be possible. Liquefaction was another option. The curator had described the process as "fireless cremation."

Emmit knew that this was the polite way of saying that lye would be poured over his mother's body and then she would be immersed in a high pressure water tank until all that remained was a small amount of brown liquid. Emmit squirmed at the idea of liquefaction, even though he knew logically that it was no less violent a process than burning a corpse to ash. That left disintegration—the process by which a body is flash frozen chemically and then shaken by a vibrating machine until it fell quite literally to pieces. The "product" was then treated and swept into an urn.

Berstwnn poked his head into the room.

"Emmit? Ah. I've just finished sending off the last of the guests. I really need to get back to the office. One can only take so long of a lunch."

He glanced down at his watch and shot Emmit a martyred look.

"If you're not *busy*, could you come help with the clean up?" As he was leaving he added, "And for God's sakes stop dodging Mr. Halifax. The poor man's been buzzing about in a frenzy."

Emmit trudged after his brother, rolling his eyes. They shared half of a genome, but Emmit had difficulty seeing any similarity between himself and Berstwnn. For one thing, they looked almost nothing alike. His brother had a shiny olive colored scalp, not entirely covered by his retreating hair—hair that was flat and brown and lifeless. Emmit was taller; his dark blond curls fell into his black-fringed eyes. His irises had none of the pale blue character of Berstwnn's; they were instead a hazel-green, borrowing a golden tint from his hair. Whatever designer genetic cocktail their mother had drawn did its job well.

The genetic diversification laws of the last few millennia mitigated the evolutionary consequences of trait selection. Though it was not mentioned in polite society, they also helped prevent accidental incest. It was bound to happen—when the average life span was eight or nine centuries, who could keep track of all those cousins? Almost no one had traditional children anymore. The risk of disease was too high, as were the tax costs of non-diversified genetic progeny.

Committed couples who wished to have children together had their genes combined (in whatever favorable way) to create one half of their child's chromosomal makeup. They then used a randomizing program to generate the other half. Many people also had children without a partner's involvement. That was how Emmit and Berstwnn came into the world, with only a mother. The donor parent simply used random material in addition to their own. Of course the genes weren't truly random. The old disease-prone areas had been glossed over. Traits that weren't generally desirable or healthy were removed. But the law required a certain degree of uncertainty. So children could still turn out short of attractive, athletic, geniuses.

Emmit's great-uncle Wynford made an excellent example. The man had spent half of the memorial service stuffing miniature quiche down his trousers. Even so, Genetic Perfectionism had led to massive social problems in the past, and no one wanted to revisit those days in the histories. The current consensus was that a diverse and evolving population was a happy one.

The curator cornered Emmit as soon as he entered the central reception chamber. Making up his mind in the instant, Emmit waved him off with an abrupt, "I think we'll go with the disintegration." Emmit turned and started gathering armfuls of decorative plastic plants and condolence cards. The curator popped up near his elbow, and, in a tone apologetic yet insistent, began, "Sir we do really need your final disposal orders as well…"

Emmit mumbled a promise to have a final answer by the next morning and dashed out. He clutched the tokens he had gathered close to his chest as he propelled past the pavilion and down the block. The second decision was by far the more difficult one of deciding what to do with the remains.

Shooting the deceased into space was most recently in vogue. Brightly colored and decorated containers were launched off into orbit, careful to avoid any important gravitational fields. *Begin the endless journey in Style!* read the advertisements for Style Space Propulsion. Emmit saw the screaming colors of their ads every day in the building in which he worked part-time. Something about drifting forever into nothing seemed bland, unless possibly you got caught in an orbit or pulled into an imploding star. Nah. His mother would have said such an exit was for overdramatic whiners.

Emmit sped along, not listening to the slow drip of water falling off the edges of the walk into the sewer channels. There was a smashed parcel of food up ahead, an offering to the street birds. Or someone had dropped his lunch. The pigeons were impressed, regardless. They made irate noises as Emmit crashed into their feast. They scuttled away but quickly returned. Emmit appreciated this brief encounter with nature. He remembered hearing stories of the animals of the old world, furry and clawed and scaly things. An animated speaker, his mother had illustrated this forgotten planet with her hands and voice. As a little boy, his mother's grandfather had even apparently been to something called a zoo. He had seen these magnificent creatures in person.

Emmit had seen pigeons and sewer rats. Also a great number of insects, but that was hardly interesting. Once he went to a friend's dinner party and met a domesticated gutter cat. It had three legs. The cat's owner had rescued him from an unfortunate drilling incident in the underground drainage projects in which she worked. It managed to get around quite well, if a bit noisily, stumping around the house with surprising speed. The whole experience was a great novelty for Emmit.

The pavement that had long since spread across the open spaces of the world had choked out what used to be green and growing. With it went the creatures that could not survive urban environments and the ever-encroaching human population. At least that's what Emmit had read. He had been on a tour of the city green-growers' building as a little child, to see where the population's food came from. But the farms were enclosed in an immense industrial warehouse, not in the open air of the agricultural fields described in historical texts.

Plants could be grown in boxes, but even genetically designed animals proved to be ill adept to survive in such. The zoos died out as quickly as its occupants had. His glum train of thought was broken by the appearance of his apartment—one of many near-identical structures. Blue-grey with rounded edges, the concrete buildings bit into the sky like so many teeth. Once he got up to the twelfth level, and into his rooms, Emmit let the contents of his arms fall haphazardly onto a table. He kicked off his shoes and collapsed into the old mushy couch. Pressing his hands into his face, Emmit blotted out the world for a moment. She was his favorite part of their family. They hadn't spoken for months before her death—he had been busy doing things so important he couldn't even remember them. Berstwnn had seen her only the week before for a family dinner. Rising up, Emmit attempted to shrug off the responsibility he felt. Feeling the empty ache in his stomach, he remembered that he hadn't eaten yet today. He walked to the kitchen.

Berstwnn had offered to pay for a notch in a nice storage building. It was simple and clean—not at all like the overwrought or garish sites that had become commonplace. Their mother would be stored in a box on a wall, one amongst thousands, accessible by a small lift in case they wanted to visit. Emmit said no. He couldn't afford such a place, and he knew Berstwnn expected a slavish look of gratitude. Emmit glowered into the frozen rice meal he was heating.

The sea was always a classic. People had been releasing the dead to the sea for as long as recorded history could remember. Of course they used to do it with actual bodies. Emmit shuddered at the thought. Magnificent creatures apparently used to roam the seas too, before life in the waters was slowly choked out by poisons and waste—the industry of men. Emmit could imagine silent deserts of ash pressed beneath the crushing waters—thousands of years' worth of the dead, forming dunes amongst their fellows. It was not very dignified. Maybe he would just put his mother into a nice urn and keep her under his ScreenVision. Emmit cracked a smile at the thought. She probably wouldn't have minded so much.

Emmit went to bed without an answer. The next morning he was woken by the sharp pokes of light entering through his windows.

He lay in bed, for an indeterminable amount of time, listening to his own breathing.

Suddenly unable to bear the sound of his beating heart for another second, he sprung out of bed. He scrubbed himself raw in the shower just to have an excuse to stop thinking. Emmit dressed slowly and ate even slower. Finally, he was unable to justify lingering, and resignedly set out for the memorial hall. The curator was not in. The pretty receptionist had instructions to collect Emmit's answer, however, and to make the arrangements. Emmit found himself back in his apartment an hour later, staring at the box under his television screen.

The seeming obsession with nation-spanning roadways and airways at the 1939 World's Fair, coupled with preparations at the time for the coming World War, gave impetus to our next story.

Cassandra L. hails from Melbourne, Australia where she writes short stories and screenplays.

Exit 5710

By Cassandra L.

Harriette slipped a cigarette between her lips and snapped the holder shut. She turned it in her fingers a while, flipping it on the pivot created by her thumb and little finger, then let it stop. It landed on the inscription on the back: *To Harrie, be good, love from your sister, J.* She ran her thumb over the letters—so familiar, so aggravating, so endearing. How much yet how little had changed over the years.

She kicked her legs against the towbar, glad for the movement. Superhighways or not, the drive from Sydney was long and she wasn't used to the truck. She'd travelled two hours before she finally felt comfortable with the weight and even then she was wary. Why they gave her the job was anyone's guess. Perhaps they'd already drained the barrel and she was the dregs. With the case back in her shirt pocket, she drew a match along the metal of the tank and lit up.

The one rule she respected was the one about smoking in the cabin. She was told she wouldn't see a single cent if they smelt even the faintest whiff inside the truck. It made for a good excuse for a break.

Smoke drifted out of her nostrils and away past the cigarette lodged in the corner of her lips. She looked up at the back of the tank: a handwritten sign stated *Caution! Chemical Load* but nothing said flammable. She wasn't too worried anyway.

A car passed, unhurried. Husband and wife, hats on their heads – retirees or tourists. Which ever it was, Harriette saw blank disinterest on their faces: whether the landscape was novel or familiar, the world inside was always the same. They had forty years or more touring together and it was evident. The wife's gaze settled on Harriette a moment too long – a gesture of judgment or envy, she wasn't sure. But then they were gone, up the on-ramp to join the other specks moving across the great aerial superhighways of the National Trans-Continental System.

It was peaceful down below the concrete pylons. Around her, roads curved in loops and whorls leading up or leading out – everything leading away from her. The earth was turning yellow as spring's bounty turned to summer's heat, but it was cool under the superhighway's shadow. In the distance sheep moved through automatic gateways, shepherded by automatons whose engines were too distant to hear. She wished she had time for a beer.

Flicking the spent butt away, she jumped off the tailgate. The ground seemed further away than she remembered, and unstable. Stars pricked at the edge of her vision. She paused and the world became solid once more; she stretched, rolled her sleeves back up, and made for the cabin.

Over the dash, the curb looked close. Harriette edged the truck around, feeling only a small bump as the back wheels grazed the edge. The load shifted then righted itself. She wiped her nose with the back of her hand and cursed her sister for living so deep in the suburbs.

Her sister's house wasn't on the itinerary, but she had time. Accommodation was part of the deal: overnight at a transfer station just out of the Melbourne area with a further pick up in the morning, then straight off to Adelaide. But she was running ahead of schedule and Jeannie was only twenty minutes away. No harm in dropping by.

It would be unannounced but not unexpected. She had called her sister from a long-distance booth in Sydney to tell her the news.

Oh yes…? had been the response: scepticism, disapproval and concern wrapped up in two simple syllables and a raised eyebrow.

"It's all above board," Harriette argued, "you think I wouldn't check?"

Her sister's red lips pressed thin, pulled at the corners – the tiny action made large on the screen on the wall. Harriette could see her two nieces playing quietly in the background.

"I didn't say that," Jeannie said. The sigh came through the line, crystal clear, as if they were in the same room. Only the noise from the street behind her broke the illusion.

She stretched her legs out as far as they could go within the booth and shifted on the worn seat; she thought to herself she should get a Visiphone unit installed in the apartment. After all, she'd have the extra money soon.

"The interview was at the depot. Had to drive a truck to show 'em I could," Harriette continued. She always had to justify herself. "Told 'em distance was no problem. Had to sign contracts and have a medical and everything."

"I just don't understand why they'd take a good pair of girl's hands away from the line," Jeannie said, "honestly, I don't."

Harriette shrugged. "I don't know either."

And it was true. She didn't. The poster pinned to the notice board near the urn in the break room gave little clue. *"Girls!"* it read. *"Do you have a driver's licence? Your nation needs your help! Sound rates of payment and accommodation guaranteed."* Harriette wasn't patriotic, but she did have debts. Silly debts. If she was a gambler or had children to care for she could understand it – but she had nothing to blame other than poor respect of money and a lifestyle above her means. The wage she received on the assembly line barely covered the repayments, once rent and company fees had been deducted. The pawnshop slip wasn't the only factor in her decision, but it held the most weight.

"Is this something to do with the war effort?" Jeannie continued. "Because I don't like to think of you getting involved in other people's business…"

"I don't know, might be," she replied. "Could be why they wanted girls 'cause the useful men are all off being useful."

"There's nothing useful in it. It's Europe's problem, what's that got to do with us?"

"The world's a smaller place now, Jeannie. Maybe it has got something to do with us?"

On the screen, the red lips pulled thin again. "Since when do you follow politics?"

"I don't, I don't know," Harriette shot back. A red light blinked near the coin slot, a count-down of ten; she was regretting spending the money. "Look, I gotta go. My first run's via Melbourne. I'll…"

Her sister's face snapped into a reflection of her own as the screen flickered to black. Mascara-tipped long lashes turned thin and mousy-blond, the delicate waved bob replaced by a simple braid. And although the lips were pale, they were the same shape, as were the nose and the brows. No matter how far their paths had deviated, how stooped Harriette became, or how many kilograms appeared on Jeannie's tall frame, they were undeniably sisters.

That was yesterday. Now Harriette negotiated the crescents and the boulevards of jejune suburbia to find her sister's bungalow. Of the rows of identical houses, their tiny deviations only served to show how much they were the same: perhaps there was a variation in the flowers planted, a different car in the driveway, a child's tricycle instead of a bicycle by the front door. But they served as poor landmarks, and Harriette concentrated on the street names to navigate: Begonia Street, Peony Crescent, Petunia Grove. Even they had their uniformity.

She sniffled, drawing back the mucus slowly trickling down her sinuses. Perhaps it was the spring blossoms, perhaps it was a sympathetic reaction to the floral street names, but the farther she drove into the suburb the worse her allergies became, though she couldn't remembered it being this bad.

She didn't mean to leave it so late. Two years passed so quickly: intentions were pushed back and weeks turned into months. There was that trip she took with Charlene and John and Tommy McKinley to the resort park at Surfer's Paradise, and that week away with Billy Chalmers, who took off back to Perth soon after. She couldn't afford more time off work after that. But to her sister, she always was 'busy' or she had 'double-shifts'. *It's more expensive up here in Sydney*, she'd say, *but I'll come soon.* It was easier than telling the truth.

The clock on the dash said 5:23. Harriette knew she could turn around at the next roundabout, head back out to the depot where she was expected to spend the night. Jeannie would be none the wiser.

She pulled into a little shopping precinct at the end of her sister's street. All the retail cubes were shuttered for the night, and not a single soul or vehicle occupied the space. She left the truck parked across several carparks and made for the row of Visiphone booths.

Inside, she paid only for the regular phone – a local call. Coughing wet into her sleeve, she paused to recover before dialing through

The operator transferred her immediately, and Harriette waited five rings before the line clicked a connection. "Hello?"

Dance music from a stereophone and laugher drifted down the line. The voice that cut through the noise was a relief to hear.

"Shelly?"

"Harrie? Is that you?"

She smiled, she couldn't help it. "Yeah, it's me. I'm in town. What's doing tonight?"

"Just a small gathering, you coming?"

"Maybe. Later," she said.

"Something on?"

"Just dinner with my sister first," she said, finally committing herself. "You'll still be there at 10?"

"Your sister? That's no fun. You definitely ought to come here after," Shelly said. Amongst the voices in the background someone called out, *Harrie's here!* "We're thinking of going out later for a lark but we're not sure yet. We'll wait for you."

"I'll see you then," Harriette said. "I've missed you."

"I've missed you too, hun . . ."

Harriette hung up before she could say goodbye.

The truck loomed large outside the rows of neat bungalows, a hulking, metal-and-rivet behemoth amongst polite, sleek sedans. Harriette felt an overwhelming tiredness and took a moment to catch her breath. At the living room window, the curtain pulled back and her sister's face appeared. There was no possibility of a surprise – she was always looking out at the world, watching for something to knit her brows over.

She was halfway up the path when the front door opened and Jeannie stood with her two daughters beside either hip. Violet tottered forward with unabashed glee, shouting *Auntie Harrie! Auntie Harrie!* while June hung back half hidden behind her mother's leg.

In one quick sweep, Harriette lifted Violet up. She leant down to kiss June on the cheek, then kissed Jeannie; as much as her sister wanted to show her displeasure at the irregularity of the visit, her eyes softened and face relaxed.

"You look dreadful," she said, a genuine note of worry under the brusqueness of the statement, "are you well?"

"Well enough," Harriette replied. "Long day on the road. Now, who wants to see the truck?" she asked the girls.

Despite the resounding cry of *me! me!* from Violet, June shrank back behind her mother's apron. "Trucks are for boys," she murmured.

"Aw, that's not true!" Harriette jostled little Violet on her hip and grabbed her nose with her knuckles. "But you'll have a look, won't you, you little vagabond?"

"Don't call her that," Jeannie said.

"Why not?"

"You know why," Jeannie warned.

Harriette knew why. *Because that's what Dad called me.*

"And the new stovetop has sensors to automatically detect the temperature inside the pan . . ."

Harriette nodded, trying to find enthusiasm yet only finding boredom. Her sister's new kitchen was impressive on one level, but entirely dull to Harriette – she'd hardly cooked a meal for herself in nearly two years. Everything hummed and whirred and steamed, and the scent of lamb and peas and gravy made it hard for Harriette to concentrate. Her gaze shifted around the chrome modules, and she noted the single wineglass sitting amongst the coffee cups in the dishwasher, remnants of red wine still liquid in the bottom.

"…it's amazing, I barely have to lift a finger," Jeannie continued. "Electricity takes care of everything!"

"Amazing, Jeannie," Harriette parrotted, "you've done really well for yourself."

Her sister beamed, "Samuel wants only the best for me." June walked silently into the room and began setting the table – only four places.

"He's not joining us tonight?" Harriette asked.

"Oh, he's away on business," Jeannie said, turning away to respond to a pot that had begun to beep its culinary victory. "Since his promotion the company has been working him so hard . . ."

June and Violet cleared the table, Violet holding the cutlery in her fat little fingers, while her sister managed the plates. June returned with two mugs dispensed from a machine on the bench – one of tea and lemon for her mother, one of sweet black coffee for Harriette.

Jeannie waited for her daughters give their aunt a kiss goodnight then file out the room. "Do I need to set up the fold-out bed?" she asked quietly once the girls were out of earshot.

Harriette shook her head and pulled out her cigarette case. "No, I'm not stopping."

"Where will you go at this hour?"

"Out," she snapped, then felt bad. "I'll visit Shelly while I'm here."

Jeannie's lips pulled thin again: every argument since the day Jeannie caught Shelly and her smoking in the toilets was writ across her face. Harriette blew smoke over her shoulder away from the table and let the matter sit heavy between them.

"You can always move back," Jeannie said. "Things aren't working out for you up there. There's no shame in it if you return. Samuel and I can help you. You're twenty-five. A girl like you shouldn't have to support herself, not at your age. You can do better . . ."

"I know," Harriette replied quietly. Her refusal to bite left them in silence.

"Will you visit Mum and Dad while you're here?" Jeannie asked eventually.

"Not this time, maybe next run," Harriette said, "Got a pick up in the morning, won't have time to get them flowers."

Jeannie nodded, non-committal, but Harriette could read exactly what she was thinking: *But you have time to visit your friends . . .*

"You still have Dad's watch?"

Harriette held her coffee close, blowing across the surface then letting the steam return. "Yeah, back home. In the safe."

The tram was new. Harriette knew the network was to be expanded before she left. She'd seen pictures of it in travel ads – sleek angular tubes transporting smiling families and salary-men from suburb to city to suburb – but this was the first time she'd seen it for herself. She was impressed.

At that hour, the smiling families and salary-men were all safely tucked away in their beds; Harriette had few fellow passengers as the tram sped along. Outside, the bungalows and prefabs gave way to commercial districts and apartments in neat blocks, growing ever taller until she was on the outskirts of the skyscraper world of the inner city.

She got off by the racecourse, under neon lit bridges and over-passes that crossed the river and lead to the port. As glad as she was to be back, she began to regret turning down the offer of the fold-out.

The noise of the stereophone drifted into the street. At the townhouse door Harriette was greeted by tight hugs, alcohol-infused shrieks, and a glass of cheap whisky mixed with juice pressed to her lips. Faces she hadn't seen for years, faces she had known since she was a schoolgirl, pressed into hers.

"You look so pale!" Shelly cried, squeezing Harriette's cheeks tight between her palms. "Are you alright?"

The scrum shifted them to the living room to where more faces waited around the speakers. Shelly pointed at the new ones by way of introduction. "…and this is Cheryl, and Olivia, and this is Billy…"

Billy looked up with something that might have been a smile in his eyes. "Alright, Harrie?"

The drinks flowed and the group moved on from Shelly's town-house. The city buzzed through the late-night spark of its twenty-four hour cycle. They had beers in downtown bars playing feverish jazz in basements under office towers. They took glass elevators up to a rooftop jungle where they pooled their coins for bags of peanuts to throw to topless men and women who half-heartedly gambolled about like monkeys. Shelly and Olivia snuck into a all-night bottle shop and came bolting out with something wrapped in a newspaper.

The group ran screaming down towards the river. Harriette didn't have the energy to keep up, nor did she have the energy to fight Billy's arm as it wrapped around her shoulder. She wished she could be glad for his body weight; she leant into him not from affection but from sheer, glazed-eye exhaustion.

They turned into the gardens. "I thought you were in Perth," she said.

"I was," he replied.

"Now you're in Melbourne." It wasn't a question. "Did you know Shelly? Before?"

"No, no. We just move in similar circles." He looked down at her. "We worked out you were a mutual acquaintance after a while," he added.

Harriette slowed. They stood close to the bank: around them the city sparkled in light and neon, and the wide, glassy-dark water carried the sounds of the nocturnal city across its surface. "You know I really liked you," Billy said softly.

"Liked," she echoed. "Past tense."

"Maybe I still do," he continued. She could feel him waiting for her response but she had fallen beyond caring. "We're too much alike, that's our problem. We could never settle."

"I never asked you to," she said.

She started coughing and turned away from him; the dark flecks were unmistakable even in the dim night light.

"I need to go back," she said, pulling away against Billy's embrace.

"What's wrong?"

"Have to be at the depot in the morning," she said. "Tell the others I said goodbye."

Billy tugged on her shoulder, the light force nearly knocked her off balance, but still she kept walking. He was still calling for her when she reached the street and disappeared into the crowd of revellers and late-night sight-seers. They flocked around the station, with is quaint yellow nineteenth century façade and modern spherical additions. Harriette was glad to find support in their mass.

By the time she made it back to the tram she was close to sleep. A young couple, already past the initial blush of their relationship, sat down opposite her: at ease with their arms around each other, they talked quietly and laughed softly at jokes only they understood. It confused her how they could be so comfortable.

She slept the last hours of the night in the cabin of the truck. Just before she drifted off, she saw the curtains move at her sister's bedroom window up at the house. Jeannie's face stared out, a pale and naked orb that Harriette wanted to believe was full of love and concern and not disparagement.

Workmen appeared in her side mirrors as she backed the truck in. Their faces, hidden behind gas masks, told her nothing, but their body language held no secrets: Harriette was late and she'd kept them waiting. A gloved hand beckoned her towards a glassed-off office and she jumped out of the cabin.

She was asked to explain herself, which she did, and the manager didn't really care. Nor did she. Her gaze drifted as he lectured her on the importance of schedules and discipline, and her role in a bigger picture. Outside the glassed walls, men in thick rubber suits and breathing apparatus pumped more chemical load into her truck. The weight would be different again. She'd have to take account of that, she thought.

A sharp rap of knuckles on the desk startled her and brought on another bout of coughing. "Are you even listening?" the manager hissed. "You girls are worse than useless. No wonder you lot are all unmarried . . ."

Back on the open road, the manager's words dissolved and sank low into the pool of voices flowing at the back of her mind, joining those of Billy and her sister. She took the on-ramp a little faster than she should have. Her stomach dropped and her brain pressed up against her skull leaving her suspended as the truck whipped itself around with the force of its momentum. She was going over the edge and inside she felt perverse flash of relief.

The dreadful list to the left swung back and the world snapped back into place. A car's horn blared behind her: in her mirrors a man in a red sports car gave her the finger. Blinking hard to ease the burning sensation from her eyes, she pulled her attention back to the task in hand – just six more hours and she would be done.

The superhighway stretched like a beam of white light piercing the horizon. She sighed and reached for her cigarette case out of instinct but through the fog in her brain she remembered the rule. She grabbed the thermos of coffee instead.

It was the last gift from her sister. At dawn, a faint tapping against the cabin door startled her awake: outside was Violet armed with the thermos and a paper lunch bag. She let her niece climb in, both of them still slow from sleep. After she'd cleared of lungs of mucus and clots, Harriette pulled Violet towards her and let her snuggle close; the sweetness of the little girl's unconditional love brought Harriette close to tears. "Don't be like me, little vagabond," she whispered into her soft hair, "but don't be like your Mum either."

Cars passed her with numbing regularity; the memory of Violet's warm embrace disappeared. Harriette's nose ran and her lungs ached and her eyes felt gritted with embers.

Two hours from the depot, a roaring began in her ears. Her jaw clenched in response. A small tremor started in her legs, growing in intensity under the soles of her feet. She held on to the steering wheel and slowed, deaf to the horns blaring behind her. If she lost consciousness at that speed, she thought, she would go over the edge and plunge into the paddocks below. Or worse, drift across eight lanes of fast-flowing traffic . . .

She flicked the indicator and merged into the emergency lane, then pulled back out again: the roaring was replaced with a blast of a freight train's horn.

To her right, the streamlined engine thundered down the median strip, followed by shipping containers and giant drums rattled on their tracks. They seemed almost taunting and cruel in their appearance – there was no reason she could see for her to be taking this load by road and the train only served to remind her of this.

And yet she was. Another hour and she'd see the giant geometric arches welcoming her across the border to South Australia. The land underneath the superhighway would become salt-encrusted and scrubby and the soil would turn ochre. Massive water pipes would appear, lifelines stretching from the Murray River out to parched towns and fields. She would take the turn at the interchange to the Adelaide bypass until she reached Trans-Continental Exit No. 5710.

All she had to do was stay conscious and stay in her lane.

Shadows were long by the time she navigated through anonymous gateways and past stony-faced security teams. She heard the word *medic* and knew it was directed at her. A suggestion, maybe, perhaps an order. They handed the papers back and directed her on.

The depot wasn't what she expected, though she barely could register anything beyond her front grill. The world took on a crimson tinge that merged with the flat red earth. Large, low sheds clustered in small groups and she edged the truck around until she found one painted with a large number 4. She blinked. Somehow, just before her consciousness gave out, she recognised the letters printed below it: DEPT. OF DEFENCE.

When she came to, the engine was off. The angle of her head, forward against the steering wheel, caused the mucus to run freely from her nostrils and she spluttered. A pair of hands in thick gloves lifted her from under her arms, another pair pulled her legs. She was at the mercy of rubber-suited men. As they carried her away she caught sight of herself in the side mirror: her face was swollen, her eyes barely more than slits. It wasn't mucus that poured from her nose – it was blood.

The first time she woke up, there was something clamped over her nose and mouth. Something that hissed. She blinked once, then twice, slowly trying to make sense of the sensation of heat and of the firm surface beneath her back. On the third blink, she lost consciousness again.

Later, she woke properly. Memories slotted back into place again: driving, the long stretches of the Trans-Continental, her sister, Shelly, Billy, Violet . . .

"How're you feeling, love?" a voice asked. A nurse appeared, her movement belying the camouflage of her white uniform against the white tiles.

Harriette shifted slowly up onto her elbows. As her eyes took focus, she saw the tiles were cracked and edged with red dust. She was in a hospital bed, yet the room appeared set up for a duel purpose: a makeshift ward at her end, and operating theatre at the other. Green plastic dividers waited on wheeled frames.

Later that night, the dividers were drawn out and Harriette watched the shadowplay of a barrel chested soldier having his leg bones reset and plastered.

She saw him again when they let her move about. After three days, she was allowed to walk around a little. Barriers, both physical and corporeal, limited where she could go;the energy had all but been sucked from her, but for what she could manage Harriette was grateful.

She shuffled with the drip bag frame for support down tiled corridors until she found a small common room. The soldier sat on a sofa with his leg elevated, staring, expressionless, at a telescreen on the back wall. Curled on an armchair opposite was a stocky, strong-jawed girl with close cropped hair, small, dark eyes, and a cigarette between her knuckles.

"So you're our new patient?" she said. "Welcome back to the land of the living."

Harriette moved herself to a spare chair, wrangling her drip over the faded rug in the centre of the room. Even when she was blocking his view, the soldier's face remained motionless.

On the screen a slapstick variety show went through its motions. "I heard things were bad with you," the girl continued.

"Might be," Harriette said. Sweat trickled down the back of her gown; though the infirmary was brick and better insulated, the air still hung hot and heavy, baked by the harsh, unimpeded sun. The three of them sat back in silence, eyes on the screen. Nobody laughed.

"Surprised you're still with us at all," the girl said. "Took six trips before I showed my first symptoms, and that's just from incidental exposure."

"Exposure to what?"

The girl looked over at the soldier. "You going to tell her, soldier boy?" she called. He didn't react. "Top secret. No one'll tell you. Not with the war on. That's why they made us sign them papers. Still," she said, pointing her cigarette at Harriette, "you're lucky. You took a direct hit. Heard 'em talking outside your room and the term *lethal dose* was thrown about."

"What do you mean?"

"That fume leak, in your cabin. No one said anything to you 'bout that?"

"I didn't smell anything."

The girl shrugged. "You wouldn't have. Odourless, isn't it, soldier?" she said, then took another drag on her cigarette. "And carcinogenic. Bet they didn't say anything to you 'bout that either?"

When Harriette asked the nurse what *carcinogenic* meant, the nurse looked away quickly and told her not to worry about it. Then Harriette asked to make a call.

Jeannie picked up on the first ring. "Harrie! Where are you? Are you on a Visiphone?"

"No," Harriette lied. It was a duel machine, true, but she didn't think she could face her sister.

A pause. "Are you alright, Harrie?"

She took a deep breath to steady herself, but still her voice cracked. "I'm fine. I made it. I'm ok," she said. "How are the girls?"

"They're fine." Jeannie's reply was slow and full of skepticism.

"And Violet?"

"You always play favourites, just like Dad!"

"Please, Jeannie," Harriette begged. "Is Violet ok? Is she well?"

"Harriette, what are you on about?"

"Is Violet well?"

A sharp sigh rang down the line. "Yes, yes she's well. Now what's wrong? Harriette, what is going on?"

"Nothing, nothing. She just seemed sleepy this morning," Harriette said quickly. "Thanks for the lunch. Really appreciated it."

"Sleepy?" Jeannie's voice slipped upwards in pitch. "You had me all worried because my daughter was sleepy first thing in the morning?"

"Sorry," Harriette said. "Listen, I'm going to stay in Adelaide for a bit, I need you to do me a favour."

"If you need money so you can just drink it away . . ."

"No, Jeannie, please listen," she asked.

Another silence appeared on the line. Harriette had to lean against the wall for support – the military offered no soft chairs like the public Visiphone booths. "Harrie, are you crying?" Jeannie ventured.

"I need you to do me a favour," Harriette started. "I'm going to send you a slip. A pawnshop slip. I need you to get Samuel to pay it out next time he's in Sydney."

"Oh Harrie, what have you gotten yourself into now . . ."

"I need you to do this. Not for me. For you."

"For me? What are you on about?"

"It's for you. I need you to have it."

"What is it, Harrie?" Jeannie said carefully, but the hardness in her voice still seeped through. "Harrie, I'm worried. Where are you? I'm coming to get you."

"I'm fine. I'm in Adelaide. I'm with a friend. I just need you to do what I asked you to do. Please, Jeannie."

Another sigh. "You're lying to me. I don't know where you are, but you're not in Adelaide."

I don't know where I am either, Harriette thought. The closest thing to a clue she had was the little sign she could see from her window marked 'Testing Ground–Restricted'. But she did know she was miles away from Adelaide.

"So this slip, what are we picking up for you?" Jeannie continued.

"I told you," Harriette said. "It's not for me."

"What is it, Harrie?"

Her jaw trembled and her head swim. She sat herself on the floor, left arm raised to keep the drip from pulling. She could barely get the words out. "It's the watch. Dad's watch. Get Samuel to pick it up. You have it."

"Oh Harrie . . ." Jeannie started, her voice now thick too. "He left it to you and you hocked it . . ."

"Please, Jeannie, you have it, and keep an eye on Violet. Make sure she's ok," Harriette said, then added, "Jeannie, I love you."

She hung up before Jeannie could reply.

Through her bleared vision she saw the outline of a man against the white, tiled world. He approached and lifted her up gently, and she recognised him as the doctor. She blinked and his features became clear; his expression was kindly but grave.

"Come on, Miss Barker," he said. "Let's get you back to your room. I'd like you to be sitting down for what I have to say."

She rolled her weight forward, transferring it from the doctor to the drip pole. He tried to take her arm and she shrugged it off: she would walk, with what little strength she had left to her, on her own.

Our next story presents, in a somewhat sardonic tone, an image of the future. It's a future where the promise of automation has done its job, perhaps too well.

For Mr. Chandos, thoughts of the future are not unfamiliar, for he recently retired from a long career with the United States Air Force Space Command.

Master of the Underworld

by Michael Chandos

"Hold that line! Phase in the TCS."

Robots and men stood at their test stations, intent on banks of dials, rows of switches, and levers lined up like marching soldiers. Lights flashed, printouts curled on the floor like ancient scrolls, circular graphic plotters recorded flows at a hundred points. Doctor Edson Delgettis, spry and intense, 70 years old, but dynamic as a quarter horse, yelled out orders like the captain he was.

"Careful. Monitor the levels and the outputs. Phase in the carriers now. That's it, that's it! Watch out for the crossover! Key in the recycling plants. Don't let the voltage lag. Watch the flow!"

Dr. Delgettis slid about the large control station floor on his personal steel and leather office chair. It was fitted with larger diameter wheels with ball bearings that enabled him to scoot between test stations on the polished concrete floor like a jet-propelled ice skater.

Everywhere Delgettis zoomed, two Master Robots followed. A tall blue cylindrical bot, named One, was with Doctor Delgettis constantly. It was the primary data interface and control bot, and it had basic speech reproduction. Multiple actuators and arms circled its torso and its small hard wheels worked well on the concrete floor. One's main arm clutched the TCS Final Test Plan, ready for Delgettis's reference.

Two, an orange squat cylinder with three folded-up arms, had large pneumatic wheels so it could go anywhere to check utilities developments on the spot. For example, Two could be dispatched to a sewer failure and its electronic eyes would show Delgettis what was happening live through the miracle of television. It had excellent speech reproduction and reasonable speech understanding. Two often spouted progressive slogans to pump up the test team's morale.

"Steady now, steady now," said Delgettis.

Switches clicked, plotters scratched and printers clacked, but no one spoke. Delgettis stopped in the middle of the room. He leaned forward and observed his realm intently. It was all working to the Plan! The Total Control System was assuming control of all Middleton utilities for the first time!

"Hansen, what's the flow to Middleton?"

"One hundred forty five per second, flowing steady with less than two percent variance," said Hansen. He lowered his hands and stepped back. TCS was running things now. Large television monitors on his console showed pumps and reservoirs at ten different stations serving the Middleton zone. All lights were green.

Abruptly, a light flashed yellow and almost immediately went to red. The engineer sprung to the console.

"No," said Delgettis. "Wait to see if TCS catches it."

Knobs turned by themselves and lights flashed in cybernetic sequences. The key light went to yellow, flickered, and then to green.

"Excellent!" said Delgettis.

Two played inspirational march music and said, "A vivid tribute to the American scheme of living."

The engineer stepped back and surveyed the entire twelve-foot tall board. Satisfied, he nodded to Delgettis, who nodded in return and relaxed in his chair. Hansen looked at the other engineers. He nodded at them, and they all stepped back to let the ControlBots run the show.

Looking like short, rounded refrigerators, the ControlBots were built into slots in the consoles and were connected via thick interface cables. Interchangeable and extremely reliable, they were in charge of the Utilities Control Room now.

———

Dr. Edson Delgettis sat at his broad, mahogany desk on a raised dais. Personal monitors next to his desk mimicked critical TCS and Utilities functions. One and Two waited to the left, recharging.

The back wall of the oval control room was entirely made of windows. They overlooked the Middleton valley, the reconfigured farms and the new superhighway.

All the human engineers were arranged in a line as Dr. Delgettis addressed them.

"TCS has passed its rigorous tests and it performed flawlessly through the initial operation period. Testing has been completed. It is the dawn of a new day!"

"A new city organized to make cooperation possible between machines and men," commented Two.

"You are all being released to important tasks that need your expertise and experience. I could not have succeeded, uh, we could not have succeeded, without your expert assistance and tireless labors. With TCS, Utilities men labor no more! Thank you."

The men smiled and patted each other on the back. They engaged in small talk as they filed out the metal control room door carrying briefcases and duffle bags, and into the waiting ElektroBus.

"Hansen, wait a moment," said Delgettis. Hansen stopped in front of the desk. "Have you registered the work order to have this Control Room reconfigured?"

"Yes, Doctor Delgettis. The Workforces will be here this afternoon to remove all the desks, test equipment and other furniture on the main floor. Domestics will be here tomorrow morning to clean and polish the floor and to bring in the furniture you requested, including the couch-bed and the food unit. Was there anything else, sir?"

"No, Hansen. That will be all. Good luck running the water conversion plant. I am sure you will do well there. A future TCS site, perhaps, eh?"

"An aeration plant purifying the ground water and distributing it for hundreds of miles," said Two.

Dr. Delgettis stood up from his desk and scanned the humming control room wall. It was curved so he could look at it all in one sweeping glance. It was twelve feet tall and sixty feet long, painted a pleasant sea green and full of all the controls needed to manage and regulate sewage, clean water, electricity, storm water and natural gas for a 20,000 square mile area. His mouth curled into a subtle, satisfied smile.

"I did this," he said. TCS was *his* design.

"The imagination and vision of men who do new things," said Two. A graduation march played at low volume.

Dr. Delgettis walked to the windows. "The World of Tomorrow was predicated on a return to the natural: small, comfortable cities connected by efficient transportation, with better agriculture and better systems to relieve men of drudgery and to allow them to soar to their potential."

"The advantages of living in a small town are within easy reach," said Two.

"But, no one considered *how* it all works. No one, except me!" Delgettis's voice amped up. One and Two rolled closer.

"Not just technology, but the right technology at the right time to solve the right problems. Sprung from man's industry and his genius," said Two, always the sycophant.

"This success is mine!" yelled Dr. Delgettis.

"A triumph of individualism in a battle of wills against the old methods!" proclaimed Two.

One held up the TCS Test Plan as though it was a sacred prayer book.

" The highways get all the press," complained Delgettis. "And the new efficient cities running on streamlined principles, get the honors. Better lives for everyone. Humpf. My design is Art!" Delgettis turned to the control consoles.

"Highway engineering at its most spectacular," said Two. "All the highways of all research and all the activities of science lead us onward to better methods of doing things and better ways of living." A stirring symphony by Aaron Copeland replaced the march music.

"It all needs power to run. I bring them that! I warm their homes with natural gas. I clear the human waste no one wants to think about. And I do it all underground. Automatically and reliably. Gone are the ugly telephone poles. Gone are the smelly sewers."

"Gone! The children need the Earth for playing and growing," said Two.

"And TCS controls it all, without the need for human labor."

"No humans," said Two.

"The machine is me and I am the machine."

"You are the machine?" asked One.

"It works because I command it! It responds to me and to me only. I am the designer. Me, Delgettis!"

"Bel Geddes? The Designer?" asked One.

"Yes, I am the designer."

One's actuators twitched and its lights spun with colors. Two was quiet as it considered what One had to say.

TCS was a marvel. It corrected errors automatically and efficiently regulated the water that children drank and the electricity that ran the televisions. It did it with minimal maintenance. It became boring.

"One, I could not ask for a more efficient and trustworthy assistant. You keep the ControlBots running day and night, switch them out when needed, adjust tasks to loads, everything. I just wish you could play cards."

"I can search the Networks for a movie you like, Designer," said Two. "The football season should start soon."

"No, thank you. I just need more stimulation."

"Would you like to solve quadratic equations again, Designer? You never finished the last ones. Remember, you shut down early last time?" said Two.

"You mean I fell asleep? Humans do that," said Delgettis. "Sometimes, I think I need companionship." He slumped in his chair.

"You are part of the machine. You are the Designer. We are maintenance and operations. We will tune you up," said Two. Both Master Robots stopped moving; they were communicating. Two then hurried out the Control Room door, sealing it behind him to not disturb the air conditioning. One rolled back to the consoles. An actuator arm extended and he fiddled with controls.

Sometime later, an alarm went off. Delgettis, asleep on the couchbed, instantly snapped awake. He rushed to the Control Room console, scanned the changing lights and grabbed a printout.

"One, what's the matter with the Anderson junction pumps?"

"Overheating. Replacement scheduled next week. No cause for early termination," said One.

"Cycle the backups. We need to be synchronized or the pressure pulse will blow the main lines. Are you ready?" said Delgettis, obviously stimulated. "Turn! Adjust! That's right. Good."

He stepped back. The printer pushed out a summary report and then stopped.

"Lights all green. Your solution is successful, Designer," said One.

"Yes. Interesting. I'll have to look into this. Send the summary data to my monitors, One." He grabbed the printout and went to his desk.

"Yes. You are the Designer."

———•••———

Two returned two days later. Dr. Delgettis's eyes were red and he needed a shave. He'd been up all night investigating the junction pump problem, but he looked happy.

"Two, where have you been? We had an interesting problem last night."

"Designer, in your best interest, I have furnished companionship."

Delgettis looked up from the data printouts. "What?"

The doublewide Control Room doors opened and a TransBot rolled in with a wooden shipping box, three feet on a side, on its low-riding dock.

"What is this?" asked Delgettis, coming down from his dais to the crate.

"Companionship, Designer," said One.

"Your stimulation is essential to the efficient operation of TCS," said Two.

"Well, eh, open it up," said Dr. Delgettis.

One extended several actuators to lever the top; two larger arms steadied the crate. The lid popped off with a scream of receding nails.

"Oh my God! What is that smell?" Delgettis looked into the crate. "Dammit, One, get that lid back on! Instantly!"

One slammed the lid on the crate, a little crooked.

"Two, what have you done?"

"You said you desired companionship, Designer. I had some shipped in," said Two.

"Oh, you damned robots!" said Delgettis. "There's a human in there. A man. A dead man!"

" The depot didn't have companionship in their catalog, so I had to special order it, said Two. "Is this not what you wanted?"

"Send this away. Now!"

The TransBot and its cargo buzzed out the doors, which immediately closed. One and Two rolled up to Dr. Delgettis.

"Robots, yes, I said I'd like some companionship, but not shipped in like spare parts. People are alive! Search your knowledge bases for the definition."

"We have erred, Designer?" said One.

"We will submit to immediate recalibration and adjustment, Designer," said Two. Both Master Robots rolled up the ramp to the dais and plugged into the special console that serviced them.

"I appreciate the effort, none the less," said Delgettis. "A woman would have been better," he muttered to himself.

One continued to fiddle and interesting problems continued to appear. Dr. Delgettis did trend studies on the service life of sewage turbo pumps. He designed a test process to monitor clean water purity and he modified the way roads and utility tunnels interfaced.

One day, Two appeared with another surprise.

"Who is this woman, Two? Madam, are you lost? Can I call an ElektroCab for you?" said Delgettis.

Two led in a woman of retirement age, well dressed, in a country way, with several suitcases.

"A new companion, Designer," said Two. "She plays cards."

"I answered an ad for a companion. What kind of a Doctor are you?" she said. Her voice was pleasant enough, if a little creaky.

"I am the Director of Utilities Systems for this Zone," he said. "I am an architect and structural engineer by education, both to the Doctorate level; the designer of the systems you see in this room, in fact."

"Where do you live?" she said. "Where is your home?"

"Here, in the Control Room. It meets my needs."

"Oh." She looked around the cold, industrial Control Room. Delgettis had converted one corner into his living area. The couch-bed was pulled out, not made up, the food unit needed cleaning and dishes were piled near the sink. Stacked crates were his closet and chest. "Perhaps you could call me an ElektroCab."

"One, I appreciate your work to find me companionship. Female was a better idea. Especially alive."

"A better idea for today and a foundation for tomorrow," said Two.

"Perhaps someone younger, a graduate student or a Post-Doc?" asked Delgettis.

"Continually striving to replace the old with the new," said Two.

"Perhaps I should go to Middleton and look for someone myself. Please call me an ElektroCab."

"Can't leave," said One. One stopped the calibration it was doing and approached the dais.

"No Designer. You are an essential component of the TCS machine. You cannot leave," said Two.

"It would be much more efficient for me to go out and select my own companion," said Delgettis. "Call an ElektroCab. I'm leaving."

"The Control Room doors are always locked, Designer," said One.

"To avoid interruption and to encourage better levels of concentration," said Two.

"I am the Master here! Get out of my way!"

"If you were ever broken, TCS and the mission here would be in terrible jeopardy. You are an irreplaceable component of TCS," said Two.

Delgettis rushed back to the consoles at his desk. "I will reset you both!" He initiated a sequence of commands, flicking switches and pulling the main power breaker. Nothing happened.

"Millions depend on the reliable completion of our tasks at the Utilities Control Room. There is no backup. We are on duty continuously," said Two. "Please resume your assigned tasks."

"I…I'll phone out!" he said.

"We can grow a companion for you, Designer," said Two. "We can apply advanced science and new industrial methods to design the companion you need."

"What? That's totally absurd."

"You, as Designer, specify the qualities you need and we, the maintenance machines, meet those needs. Physics and chemistry have joined hands with humankind in helpful friendship," said Two. "A companion molded to your human wants."

One went back to the console, attending to a ControlBot. Two headed for the Control Room doors. An arm extended an arc welder head.

"Machines become more automatic and the men who govern them more human. This new age builds a better kind of social structure molded to human wants," said Two as Copeland played again. "New things, better things, good things for all humankind."

"I insist you unlock the doors. Please," he said. He turned and went to the solid glass windows.

"No, Designer," said One.

"Please return to your desk, Designer. That is your duty station," said Two.

"But…"

Dr. Edson Delgettis, a vital component of the machine that was the World of Tomorrow, slowly returned to his desk and sat down.

"It is where you belong," said One. "It is better."

"We will make a greater world, a better world, a world that will always grow forward," said Two, and took up his station in front of the Control Room doors. "A new way of living."

Our second story featuring Elektro, comes from Australia, where William Stanforth writes screenplays and short stories, with a collection titled, "Bad Nostalgia" forthcoming.

Mr. Stanforth drew from archival footage of Elektro performing at the World's Fair and caused him to ponder a world where such automatons are commonplace. We often read how robot helpers may make life easier and more productive. But is that necessarily so?

Elektro The Westinghouse Moto-Man and Me

by William Stanforth

The living room is filled with a thick haze of cigarette smoke. It billows from Elektro's once bright gold mouth and sits like a fat cloud above us. My eyes sting and I have to squint to see the television.

He seemed almost human when I bought him. Now he sits around counting to five on his fingers and smoking more-or-less constantly. It's getting old. The other day, I asked him to help clean up and he just kept asking, "Who? Me?" as if there were someone else in the room. I had to lie down because I was so angry that all I could think about was smashing his big metal head in. But I resisted. I'm okay now.

I live in a small, single-bedroom apartment in a large apartment building. My neighbor's name is Bill and he is the only friend I have. I don't like him at all. Most evenings he comes around and sits on the couch with Elektro. He smokes and talks about his various conquests with women in bars and nightclubs. A year ago he somehow managed to marry a sweet, kind girl named Marie. They both live across the hall.

Bill is the slaughter floor supervisor at a nearby abattoir. Most manual jobs have been taken over by machinery and less-useless robots than Elektro. Bill is one of the few remaining people there. He says it's pretty easy work, mostly just pressing buttons and turning switches. And every now and then he and the boys find new and exciting ways to slaughter cattle. He says sometimes they trick a cow into thinking she's about to escape. The boys corner her moments before she gets out and then Bill comes at her with the pneumatic gun. Or if they get bored enough they'll just go to town on one of those poor creatures with a baseball bat and a bicycle chain.

Bill usually brings beers over and talks about the boys and the things they get up to after work: highway strip clubs, fights outside gas stations and so on. I'm pretty sure he was cheating on Marie even before they got married. It's not like I have a problem with that sort of behaviour, like I don't think I'm better than him. It's just hard to take a man seriously when he's sitting across from you and all that comes out of his mouth is real bullshit: lies upon lies, and warped justifications such as, "What does it even mean, it's just a piece of paper. Marriage is like, a word, you know?" And I don't even disagree, but it doesn't really matter what I think. I'm not the one married to him.

Elektro can speak seven hundred words. It seemed like a lot when I bought him, but it didn't take long for me to grow tired of almost everything he had to say. He's often telling me about how complex he is, and I'm not so sure anymore. I communicate with him via a telephone receiver that's connected to his torso. It's not too dissimilar to talking over the phone. You get that same sense of distance.

I guess I wanted something of a friend/butler, someone who could help me out day-to-day and maybe even be there when times got tough. As it turns out, I got neither. But I notice his presence. It's more that I was hoping for something different, and I'm frustrated that I have to keep buying him cigarettes just so he can watch television and talk about how great he is, and count to five on his fingers like I give a damn.

There is a knock on the door and I walk through the cloud of smoke to open it. Bill stands in the hallway with a six-pack of beer. He says, "Hey buddy," and then walks right past me and sits next to Elektro. I almost close the door before realizing Marie is in the hallway. She stands nervously outside her apartment with a bag of groceries and fumbles with her keys. I invite her inside and she says, "No, I wouldn't want to intrude," but finally she comes in after I insist.

Bill doesn't even seem to notice her. He's already had a few drinks with the boys and is in an agitated mood. Occasionally Marie will say something and he'll just talk over her – or if he does hear her, he'll turn the conversation into something about himself. I can see sadness in her eyes. I mostly say nothing, and as usual, Elektro smokes and tells us about his forty-eight electrical relays.

After an hour or so, Marie tells Bill she's going home to fix supper. She leaves without saying goodbye, and Bill stays and tells me about a woman he met outside a diner the other night and how he'd, "Really like to nail her."

He eventually finishes the last beer and leaves. I spend the rest of the evening on the couch with Elektro. We watch reruns of *Revenge*, a reality television series that gives victims of assorted crimes the resources to enact revenge on those who have wronged them. The last episode we watch follows a woman whose husband was killed by a drunk driver several years earlier. The producers of the show give the woman an opportunity to confront the man while he's on a date with a girl he met shortly after his release from prison. The plan is to throw a bucket of pigs' blood on the driver as he attempts to woo his date. I drift off moments after she hurls the bucket while shrieking, "Pig!" at the top of her lungs.

I hear a loud scream in the middle of the night coming from Bill's apartment. It takes me a second to realize it's Marie. She yells, "No, Bill! No!" and then there is silence.

Elektro sits motionless on the couch. I ask him if he wants to investigate and he just looks at me and says, "Who? Me?" Then I hear a door swing open and running footsteps in the corridor. Bill screams, "Stop! Come back here!" and slowly the sound fades away.

I get back into bed and around twenty minutes later there is a loud knock at my door. I hear Bill mutter something and I lie silently. Seconds later I hear heavy footsteps and a door slamming.

I think about Marie running down the dark streets in the icy night and Bill at home spinning in his selfish rage. Then I try not to think about anything at all.

The following day as I leave for work, I ask Elektro if he'd like to see a movie with me in the evening. He considers this for a moment and then begins talking about all the tasks he is capable of doing but really never attempts. I walk out the door before he has a chance to finish speaking.

During the day, I handle complaints for Metropolitan Energy. I work in the call centre and spend pretty much every minute on the telephone. Most of the time I deal with people who've had their power cut off because they haven't paid their bills. Every now and then someone who isn't a customer of ME will call and abuse me for something unrelated. Last week a woman claimed her neighbor was stealing her trashcans. I said I could be of little assistance, as waste management is run by a completely different and unrelated company. She scolded me for taking sides, then told me to go die somewhere before she hung up.

I spend most of the day thinking about Marie screaming, and I wonder where she is. I contemplate calling her, but fear it may aggravate the situation.

In the afternoon, I take almost thirty minutes of unbridled rage from a customer whose electricity bill is slightly higher than the previous quarter. He eventually wears himself out and lets it go, not before telling me about the plans he has for members of my family, specifically my mother and also my non-existent wife. He takes a few breaths and then casually says, "Alright, see you," and then hangs up. I pack my briefcase and head home.

Later, I prepare supper and then sit on the couch with Elektro. I ask him about his day and he talks about how he can distinguish red and green light with his photoelectric eyes. Only on very rare occasions will he respond to something unrelated to his own interests.

There is a knock on the door. As I make my way through the living room I briefly fantasize about Marie being on the other side. In the fantasy she tells me that Bill has left and has vowed never to return. This illusion is of course stripped away as quickly as it occurred, and I open the door to see Bill in the hallway. He cradles bottle of whiskey and sways back and forth. It looks like he's been crying. I ask him what's wrong, but I already know and don't particularly care.

"She's gone," he says, "she's never coming back." He allows himself in and makes his way to the couch. He takes the cigarette from Elektro's mouth and inhales. "She found out about the girl from the diner and left me. We didn't even do anything, but there's no convincing Marie."

I tell Bill to calm down and begin listing clichés that might be of some assistance to him: "There's plenty more fish in the sea, it's not the end of the world," and so on.

He hands the cigarette back to Elektro and says to him, "I wish I could be more like you... you don't even know what it's like to have a heart. Your life must be as easy as it gets."

Elektro says nothing and I'm unsure how he feels about it.

Eventually Bill starts to relax. He gets three quarters through the pint of whiskey and says to me, "I guess you're right, it's not so bad... you know what? It's good that it happened. I'm free now."

He decides to celebrate by taking Elektro and me to a local brothel. Elektro has no interest in women and I can't afford to pay for sex even if I could muster up the spirit. Bill says, "Well, I guess I'm screwing for three then," and picks a US hooker, a girl from

Russia and one from Cambodia. The girls escort Bill down a red-lit, empty hallway, while he declares wildly that he's a man of the people.

I get a phone call the next day at work from a woman enquiring about her increased rates. I explain to her that there are many factors contributing to jumps in electricity prices, for example the costs involved with providing customers with energy also rise.

She says, "I understand," which immediately takes me aback. I ask her if there's anything else I can help with. She pauses for a moment and says, "Please don't judge me," and then hangs up.

Later I arrive home and find Elektro on the couch with an empty packet of cigarettes. I hand him a fresh one and he looks unusually grateful – as if he didn't know it was coming.

There is a knock on the door and I discover Bill and Marie on the other side. Bill has one hand on Marie's shoulder and the other is holding a bottle of sparkling wine. I invite them both inside and they take a seat next to Elektro.

Bill is in somewhat elated mood and says, "We've had some troubles, but life is good, you know? Name one problem in this world that can't be worked out, just one thing?"

Marie forces a dead-eyed, smiling expression, and I think about how I could name at least one problem if I had the energy.

We spend the evening playing charades. Elektro and I are on the same team and we fail miserably, which actually works out as Bill is a particularly sore loser and does not take defeat gracefully. After the game, Marie announces she is getting sleepy and heads home. Bill sticks around for another hour and explains that in Marie's absence he managed to hook up with the woman from the diner during his lunch break, "We did it in one of the meat lockers up against a rack of beef chuck," he says, smiling wickedly. "When the cat's away, the mice will play."

Bill leaves and I think about him and Marie lying in bed together. I wonder if he feels bad at all, and I start to wonder if maybe she's just a little simple. I wonder what it means if she isn't simple, what that says about people in general. If she isn't, I decide that this world probably isn't suited for people who have enough courage to give a damn about anything – for those with any mild sense of dignity, or those who can't just switch off like Elektro.

I guess what I'm saying is that most people are like Bill, and me. It's not like I'm out there helping anyone. The night I heard Marie screaming I did nothing. And I don't know why.

Maybe, like Elektro, things such as courage weren't programmed into people like me. I sit around and take the nonsense quietly. Maybe I don't fight it because at my core is pure laziness.

I think people like Marie have a kind of inbuilt indestructability, but the Bills in this world significantly outnumber them. The lazy and weak, the ones like Elektro, The Westinghouse Moto-Man and me, also outnumber them – the ones who expect nothing and do nothing as a result.

I am not sure, however, about Bill saying Elektro has no heart. Maybe he does, but it's just not a very good one. Who is to say that all human hearts are the same? I've met people who have done things that'd make Elektro seem like a saint, simply because he does nothing. In a sense, his ineptitude upholds a kind of pathetic, dithering human spirit. His failure to be cruel puts him higher than the Bills in this world. But not much higher.

I wonder what life will be like in the future. I picture a world overpopulated with moto-men like Elektro. Lazy, gold metal men all smoking and talking about the things they could do. I wonder how it might differ to the world I live in now. Maybe it wouldn't be so bad. It probably wouldn't be that good either.

But I would say something like that.

The trepidation a young man feels when meeting his soon to be spouse's parents is not diminished by advances in science and technology. Instead, it can be more acute in a world where teleport booths remove the safety of distance.

Mr. Pedersen's short stories have appeared anthologies from Scarlet Galleon Publications, Emby Press, Villainous Press, and many others.

One Step Forward

By Matthew Pedersen

We got to the Transportitron Hub about a half an hour later than we should have. That irked me, but Jim never really was good at sticking to a schedule. The hover-cab set us down outside the huge, bubble-like building. I flashed my card, paying our balance as well as giving a sizeable tip. I never did understand why you should tip a robotic cabbie, but I did notice that it's glowing visual sensors became a bit less intense in response. The bot rolled out of the driver's seat and helped us with our luggage, making me feel a little better about the tip. After that it barked a "goodbye" in binary, leaving us alone with the thousands of other people pouring in and out of the Hub.

Jim groaned at the sight of so many diverse people brought together by the most modern of technologies. "I hate crowds so much."

"Try to walk off your disgust, man." I struggled to get a grip on my suitcase that was both firm and comfortable. "We'll be here the whole of twenty minutes…"

"Yeah, twenty minutes spent with a bunch of sneezing, coughing, disease riddled…" I tuned him out after that. I glanced around as I climbed the steps to the Hub's front entrance. People were everywhere I looked, each and every face looking haggard as they moved in lines from one place to another. Few of them stopped to look at some of the trees and shrubs that were planted in small patches of grass to the sides, their leaves having been trimmed to form cubes, spheres, and occasional spirals. While you wouldn't know it from the way people were acting it was a really nice day. The sun was shining, and not in an oppressive, "bake the concrete beneath your feet" kind of way. No, it was cool and breezy.

The perfect day.

I found myself hoping that things would be half as nice as that when we finally passed through the transportitron to Iowa to visit Cindy's parents. She'd gone on ahead of us a week early, just to sort of get her mom and dad… prepared. They still didn't know we were engaged, which was understandably a big deal. I didn't have much worries in regards to her mom, I mean she was a nice lady most of the time. Her father however was one of those… "drinks beers in his SUV while blaming all his problems on the advancement of technology" sort of guys. I also vaguely remember him calling me something unflattering last time Cindy and I visited them a year ago. Oh well, maybe I was wrong. Maybe he just has some really strong feelings about "figs".

We came to the entrance and stepped inside the Hub, a wall of cold air striking my face. The air-conditioning was cranked up in the entire complex. I suppose I should be thankful for that, with the constant press of people inside it probably would have become uncomfortably warm and stale without the constant, thrumming coolers. The immediate sensation however was one of discomfort. I think I heard Jim complain about it, but he was mumbling so whatever scathing comment he had to make was drowned out by the background hum of a thousand private conversations.

The glass dome that topped off the Transportitron Hub, made out of dozens of octagonal windows stacked on top of each other, kept the massive chamber naturally lit. Other than the slight temperature change it was just like being outside. I took the time to appreciate that the sun did sparkle and shine off some of the windows above, a small and unappreciated show.

"Which way's our transportitron?" Jim asked, this time at an understandable volume.

I looked around, this time closer to the floor, and saw a sign hanging from two long, thin tethers. "J-2" was painted in tight, black script on its white surface. "That's it," I said, pointing it out, "let's get going."

We walked along, out of the main press of bodies. The lines for places like New York City, Paris, England, and Las Vegas were packed tightly and moving at a snail's crawl. There were just a few loners and groups of families moving down the J-2 path. I guess Des Moines, Iowa wasn't really that happening of a vacation spot. I just kept walking, trying to ignore how much this trip was going to suck. People ahead of me moved at a more hurried pace, probably eager to get to what was most likely their Midwestern home and get the unpack. I moved at a pretty leisurely pace, trying to increase the amounts of seconds before I saw the grizzled, unwelcoming face of Cindy's father.

Off to the left was one of those automated moving walkways. I sighed at the sight, wondering just what sort of lazy person couldn't even be bothered to-

Then I saw Jim on it...

"Something wrong with your legs?" I asked, picking up my pace to keep up with him.

He looked at me nonchalantly, one hand pushing on the rail of the walkway. "Nothing, what's wrong with your brain?"

I glared at him. "Excuse me?"

"Why are you walking when there's a machine put here so you don't have to?" He asked, a smirk forming on the corners of his mouth.

"Because I am capable of moving my legs and supporting my own weight!" I said angrily. "That's there for people who are physically challenged, not for you to be lazy."

Jim put his hand to his mouth, clearly stifling a laugh. "Thanks for that Grandpa, now can you tell me all about 1939? When did you finally piece together that Hitler was a no-goodnik?"

"You're really going to stand there, literally, and contribute to the downfall of human society?" I asked.

"Downfall of society? What the hell are you talking about Tom?"

"I mean what you're doing right now is just one small piece of a horrifying puzzle! It's no different than someone driving around in a parking lot for an extra fifteen minutes looking for a spot closer to a store, or someone microwaving a gross, chemical laden TV diner every day of the week rather than taking the half hour it takes to make a proper meal. You're using technology to get out of the most minute amount of effort, rather than its intended purpose."

Jim straightened up after that remark, and the one eye visible past his long, black hair became hooded. "Exactly what is the point of a machine other than to reduce the amount of effort we, the users, are required to exert?"

"I… That's not the same thing at all—"

"—Nope, let me stop you there Mr. Big!" He thrust his arms up. "Even the most simple, easy to construct machines, as defined by a bunch of weirdos back in the far off era of the Renaissance, were only so we could finally afford the luxury of laziness. Ever hear of the pulley? How 'bout a little thing called the Lever? Or try to wrap your mind around the goddamn wedge!" He was shouting at this point, which I think drew a couple of people's eyes towards us.

It didn't help that seconds later he threw his hands up into the air, continuing his counter-rant in what I think was a really bad old time preacher voice. "All of these fantastical, mindboggling contraptions were made just so we could finally grow fat and go entire days without moving five feet. Our sybaritic lifestyles, for which we have machines like the ro-butler and the automatic lawnmower to thank for, is a stab in the eye for the cruel god who slapped us down on a giant, spherical rock surrounded by things that could easily kill us. We rose above those awful, hunter-gatherer days to build cars and planes. I get to say that my grand-papa is still alive today, and not dead because his asshole horse decided to kick him in the hip at the age of forty-nine. Not only that, but we put those fossil fuel leeching planes and auto-mo-cars to the sword. Now we have hovercars that run on recycled french fry oil and transportitrons that run on… damn it, I don't know. Magic? They probably run on magic!"

A portly, Midwestern family stared at us as I continued following Jim. "First of all, there's a compressed nuclear generator us generating enough power to tear a doorway from one hub to another. Secondly, fine… You can continue to take the easy way out and skip walking. Why don't you just get your legs chopped off and put a hover-pad where your ass used to be?"

Jim glared at me for a few seconds after that, then just started laughing. "Oh, I can't stay mad at you when you're looking at me with that indignant face. So quit being a dick and hop the ramp already, Mr. Uses-His-Legs is looking a bit flushed."

I was about to deny that, standing by my principles and walking the rest of the way to the transportitron, but the bastard had a point. The combination of keeping up with the freaking conveyor belt he was on and yelling at him had left me pretty out of breath.

"Fine," I said with a sigh, grabbed the rail and leapt over it in one quick motion. Jim stepped out of my way, letting my feet land right beside him. I was about to tell him that I was still against his use of the automated walkway, when a loud siren screamed to life.

The walkway came to a sudden stop, almost sending us falling to the floor. We managed to keep our balance, though Jim did stretch out my shirt a bit when his hand came clutching at it. Pretty soon a small, spherical drone floated up to us.

"Ticket Holder J-2-55643!" it shrieked in a loud, mechanical voice. Startled as I was, I was still had enough presence of mind to know that that was my ticket number. "Please be advised to minimize weight applied against the Leisure-Trax Motorized Walkway. Excess pressure may lead to motor degeneration and eventual malfunction. In that event, walkway use would be prohibited for machine repairs, inconveniencing your fellow travelers. This reprimand has been noted in your visitor file, thank you."

After that the sirens stopped, the drone flew away, and the walkway started up again. I hunched up, trying to make myself as small as possible as we slid along. If everyone wasn't looking at us before they certainly were now. The amount of embarrassment I felt at that moment was easily equal to anything I went through in my thirteen years or so of public schooling.

"Wowzers, I always had you pegged for a law breaking rapscallion." Jim gave me a light punch in the arm.

"Just… just shut up. I just want this day to be over with." I rubbed my eyes to try to suppress a migraine I felt developing.

"Well, try to think of it like this!" Jim began. "Nothing your father-in-law can do could be as bad as pissing off the Transportitron Hub security drone. Hmm, Transportitron. You know it occurs to me how dumb that name is." "He's not my father-in-law yet, he's just Cindy's big, scary dad. And what do you mean?" I asked, finally processing the second part of his ramblings.

"Well, the Transportitron is basically a big teleporter, right? Why not just call it a freaking teleporter, instead of throwing 'tron' at the end of transport. Sounds like something out of a sixties cartoon or something… "

"I never bothered to think about it." I sighed.

There was a silence for a while, the only sound the constant sound of the walkway's many moving gears and motors. "You're really stressed about this visit, huh?" Jim asked.

"No duh." I griped. "And I'm seriously wondering why I decided to bring you… "

I felt bad immediately after saying that, but to Jim's credit he didn't skip a beat before responding.

"Because you want as many people around as possible because you think it helps dampen down Old Man Hoffmon's displays of contempt for you." Then he reached out and pinched my cheek. "And because you just love me to pieces, yes you do!"

I slapped his hand away. "Cut it out!"

"Yeah, alright Mr. Grumpy." He leaned against the rail, and after a while I leaned against the one opposite of his. "You know, I'm not really sure why you want to get married anyways. I mean the whole domestic thing just seems a bit, gross to me. What are you going to do in a few years when she finally gets her teaching degree anyways? Move to one of those crappy suburb towns on the moon? Screw that. Like I want to live on a place that looks like my ex's ass."

"We're not going to move to the moon. We'll probably just find an apartment or something until we scrounge up enough money to find a house somewhere nearby. Although I did hear they're putting down AstroTurf all along the moon's surface now… " I added, somewhat absentmindedly.

"Oh, because that's better," said Jim, sarcasm just oozing out of his mouth.

The walkway stopped again, though it didn't bother us this time because we had our hands against the railing. Jim smirked at me and I glared back. "This time I didn't do anything!"

Before he could say anything we were on our way once again, coming closer and closer to the shining, flashing ball of energy that we were meant to leap through. Ten minutes passed, most of which we spent in silence, and the walkway stopped two more times. Admittedly I was starting to get nervous. The only reason I'd known that whole 'compressed nuclear reactor' thing was because I had read up almost everything there was to know about Transportitrons.

Something about sending each and every one of your molecules hurtling through an energy tunnel just set me on edge. It was mostly safe though, statistically… So I tried not to stress out about it too much. Unfortunately I started to feel a little queasy when we finally made our way to the front of the short line before the giant device, I started to feel a little queasy.

The robotic attendant operating the machine nodded at us, a TV screen built into what served as his head, displaying a friendly smiley face. "Welcome and standby. Your trip is about to begin, please be aware that there is a forty-six second time span between your entrance and your rematerialization at our connected facility."

"Umm… We were on the automated walkway… Was there any reason it stopped a few times?" I asked it.

"There have been some slight energy variations in Transportitron J-2's teleportation matrices. It is nothing to be alarmed about, sir."

I was about to ask some more questions, but a green light flashed and the robot gave us a short bow. "You may proceed, gentlemen. Have a wonderful day!"

"Come on, man. Haste makes waste," Jim said, and pushed me towards the bright, pulsating energy field.

I didn't even have time to protest. I just felt my face become atoms against the Transportitron, then the rest of my body shortly after. I'd been through these things before, and it was never pleasant. This time though it was worse, infinitely worse. What you usually saw when you were in-transit was nothing. Just some white light followed by whatever was on the other side. This time I saw countless colors, swirling around in awful, dazzling geometric equations. Time, space, and my own existence briefly became one then collapsed upon itself as I realized everything was one thing, and that that one thing meant nothing.

All crazy talk, but that's what happens when you're mind is converted into an incoherent energy format.

Then I was me again, just me. I had legs, and arms, and a stomach that was violently turning on me. I heard so many noises at once, one of which I think was Jim vomiting. There were people standing in front of me. One of them was a beautiful blonde girl, wearing a purple sundress. Cindy! There were also two old people, a man and a woman. Yeah, those were her parents. I was still queasy from the teleportation, and my vision focused like a tunnel towards her father.

I stumbled forward, and then latched onto his shoulders. He looked mad but I didn't give a crap. "I'm marrying your daughter." I said, and then threw up all over his shirt.

All and all, a good day.

Bobbi A. Chukran provides our next story. Ms Chukran hails from Texas where she writes short stories and tends her garden. Mainly a mystery writer these days, this is her first foray into science fiction.

The story results from her research on the Heinz exhibit at the 1939 World's Fair, where the new science of hydroponics was on display. She coupled that research with her concerns over GMO foods and wondered, what if?

Perfect Progeny

By Bobbi A. Chukran

1939

"Jeepers, would you getta load of that!" Charles Rutherford, fifteen-years old, exclaimed with excitement when he walked into the Hall of Electrical Living and gazed upwards toward the ceiling at the 25-foot high tomato plants inside individual growing domes. Each bright green, healthy plant was absolutely loaded with hundreds of red, perfectly round fruit.

Charlie was a boy who had always been fascinated by science, and he was especially fascinated by the concept that plants could be grown in water without soil. The scientists at the 1939 World of Tomorrow called it "chemi-culture."

He'd marveled at the singing and talking animated "Aristocrat Tomato Man" and a frisson of excitement ran up his spine as he realized the ramifications of such a thing. Here you could truly have a world of plenty! No more counting on nice weather or adequate rainfall to grow crops. He thought about the stories he'd heard from his grandmother about the hard times her family had gone through just to get food. If everybody would just change the way they did things, he thought, that would never be a problem again.

"Take a look at this, mom!" he said.

"For a teenager, you certainly are interested in food growing," his mother teased. "Too bad I can't get you as interested in our garden at home."

"Mom! This is different," Charlie said. "This is science. Science has found a new way to grow food! Just look at these tomato plants; they're huge! You just wait and see; science is going to make our lives so much better some day!"

His mother frowned as she stared at the plants. "I don't know about that. They can't have any real taste, can they? Not grown in soil? How can they even live?" She shook her head. "That just doesn't sound right to me. Liquid food?" She shuddered. "You won't catch me ever eating a tomato grown in water. It can't be good for a person."

"But mom!" he tried to explain. "It's called chemi-culture! They feed the plants with chemicals. And they're protected from insects, so they're ALWAYS perfect! And look how many they can grow in such a small space! There must be hundreds of plants here!"

She walked off, shaking her head. "Your grandmother would have a conniption fit if she saw this," she said, staring at the giant Tomato Man figure. She shivered. "And a perfect tomato? Who needs perfect? The taste is all that matters to me. Nothing good will come of growing vegetables like this. Trust me, son, this will never catch on."

"But mom. . ." he started.

Charlie's mother smiled down at her son and ruffled his hair. "Oh, Charlie. You're such a dreamer. Now let's go through the Electric Kitchen exhibit. I've heard wonderful things about some of the appliances there—they're all electric! Imagine that."

Charlie shrugged, not really as enthused about appliances as his mother.

"I'll bet you're eager to see the Mo-to Man and Sparko the Electric Dog," she coaxed. "I hear they're quite something. Imagine, Charlie—an electric man and dog."

He admitted that he did want to see them, but he couldn't get the Tomato Man out of his mind.

The next week, at the school library, Charlie checked out every book he could find on biology and botany, ordered abstracts of professional journal articles and got a lot more interested in his mother's vegetable garden at home. He had a lot of work to do.

1959

Charles Rutherford was having a bad day. At the age of thirty-five, he was senior chemi-culture Engineer and manager of the state-of-the-art hydro-ponics Lab on the new Air-Liner Norman Hotel #12. Somehow, an insect had accidentally flown into the vegetable lab from the adjoining flori-culture greenhouse, in spite of the double electric airlock security door system.

After a few hours, his assistant had netted the culprit—a common everyday honeybee—but not before the insect had naturally pollinated a dozen or so of Charlie's experimental tomato plants. He hoped that it wouldn't set back his current experiments in speeding up the ripening process. Over the years, he'd added his own personal methods to the chemi-culture system and had decreased the timing from the mechanical pollination of the fruit to harvest in only a few weeks. He hoped to make more strides in that area by using some new seed samples he'd ordered from a lab in Germany.

Now Charlie's emphasis was on producing the perfect tomato. Twenty-years later, he was almost there. His job in the Hydro-Ponics lab on the Norman gave him ample opportunity to carry out experiments with plenty of practical applications. For one thing, he was responsible for growing all the fruits and vegetables used in the food preparation on the massive flying hotel. With over seven hundred passengers and a large crew, he was responsible for providing thousands of pounds of vegetables every month. So far, the electrified garden kept up with the demand, but Charlie was anxious to increase production into other types of plants.

Since the enormous combination air-liner and ocean-liner, the "flying behemoth" as his wife lovingly called it, seldom landed, it took a miracle of modern science to grow all the food that life on board required. Passengers paying the princely sum of $300 for a stateroom on the flying hotel for a trip across the country appreciated the tasty, fresh food.

The lab consisted of hundreds of individual floor-to-ceiling growing tubes, each made of Plexiglas, and containing an enormous vegetable plant. Currently, Charlie was growing tomatoes, peppers, salad vegetables and exotic fruits and flowers in the on-board garden. Charlie was proud to say that the lab used an incredible amount of electricity. He had just added another vat of nutrient solution to the mixture, and was anxious to see what result it would have on the ultimate harvest.

On his days off, back on land, Charlie had a small home laboratory where he grew vegetables for his own family, and carried out independent experiments in chemi-culture. Charlie was especially fond of growing tomatoes. His home lab was much smaller, but he only needed to provide enough produce for his wife and mother. Every now and then he'd tease his mother about her vow never to eat "chemi-culture" food, but she pretended not to remember.

It was Charlie's first day off in a month, and as he was lowered to the ground on the automatic sidewalk below, he made a mental list of what he wanted to accomplish during his week at home.

His wife drove off the automated ramp and pulled over to the curb at the heli-port. "Hi sweetheart," he greeted her. "You look tired," he said, quickly kissing her and pressing a single stem of a purple rose into her hands.

"Hey, is that any way to talk to your wife who you haven't seen for a month?" Milly said, laughing, as he pushed her over to the passenger side and took the wheel. She sniffed the rose and smiled. "It smells like . . . lavender?"

"Or close. I'm still working on it. It's just one of my new experiments," he explained. "I'm sorry I said you look tired. I suppose I'm just talking about myself."

"You'll have plenty of time to relax this weekend," she said, rubbing his neck. She'd dressed casually in a yellow sleeveless seersucker top and matching pedal pushers.

He smiled over at her. "I always have plenty of time to relax. Finding things to do to keep myself occupied is the problem. It's time to find a new project. I've done just about all I can do with the tomatoes." He glanced over at her, admiring her dark hair. The yellow suited her, he thought.

In spite of the heavy traffic, they quickly drove onto the elevated speedway and were at home ten minutes later, far away from the bustle of the city. They'd moved to one of the new Town of Tomorrow sub-divisions after Charlie had secured the position with the AIR-LINER and loved their home. After a few months, Charlie's mother had moved in next door.

"So, what would you rather do with your time off? Perhaps mow the lawn?" she teased as he pressed a button in the center of the steering wheel. The garage door slid open and the engine whirred as the car rolled perfectly into the middle of the shelter. Car doors opened and they stepped out. Milly clapped her hands and the lights came on and the door slid shut.

They both knew that he'd never have to mow their lawn again since they'd purchased one of the new metal Moto-Man Lawn-keepers. One advantage of his job and his high salary, was that it allowed them to buy all the new necessities of life.

"I am anxious to see my wife," he said, and she smiled as he punched in the code to open the door to the house.

"And?"

"AND I'm anxious to check on my new plants and see how my automated electrical system is doing."

"Of course you are," she answered, laughing. "Honestly, Charlie, you and those plants. What would your mother say if she saw what you've been up to in that lab of yours?"

Charlie had wondered that himself from time to time. His mother had never seen his lab and although she knew he was growing all the vegetables they ate, she wasn't too interested in how he did it. Surely he'd proven that the food was harmless by now.

Charlie realized he was hungry and changed the subject. "So, what's for dinner?"

His wife smiled. "I put a wonderful frozen roast in my new electric cooker this morning. I was able to go out, shop *and* have lunch with the girls and I didn't have to worry about it once."

"And of course, you put lots of homegrown carrots in it, didn't you?" Charlie asked.

His wife laughed. "Of course I did. Lots and lots of carrots AND tomatoes."

Charlie laughed. "That's my girl!"

She smiled. "Honestly, I don't know what I did before we got our Electric Home Kitchen with all new electric appliances. I could never go back to doing things the old way—the way our mothers did."

Charlie nodded. "Now you're sounding like the Power Company."

They walked into the house and immediately there was a soft whirring sound and a mechanical "bark." Charlie looked down as a metal mutt made of aluminum, rivets, and gears rolled to his feet and sat down with a clunk.

Milly laughed. "Sparkler makes a great watch-dog. He always barks when those pesky electric vacuum cleaner salesmen come to the door."

"You have to admit he's handy *and* easy to care for," Charlie remarked, followed the mechanical dog into the living room and checked the temperature on a control panel beside the door leading to the conservatory.

One advantage of his new chemi-culture system was that it was fully automated, like his lab at work. At Milly's coaxing, he had designed it to look like an old-fashioned Victorian conservatory, but at the heart of it was an elaborate customized system. All-electric machines pumped the food solution through the roots of the plants in large glass containers, filtering impurities from the water. An electric probe kept the air in the room and the water at exactly the right temperature. If it got too warm, a small air-conditioner kicked on to cool it. If it got too cold, a small electric heater came on.

Of course, like his lab on the AIR-LINER, Charlie's at-home "garden" used an incredible amount of power. He frequently got congratulatory letters from the local hydro-electric company on his electricity usage.

After satisfying himself that all was well, he strolled into the kitchen. "Any mail?" he asked.

Milly nodded. "It's all on your desk. You got a very strange air-mail letter from that Olde-Fashioned seed company. It came a week ago."

"Probably want me to re-order. I'll look at it after dinner. I'm starved!" Charlie said, his mouth watering as the smell of the roast wafted through the air.

"Come and get it!" Milly said.

They sat down to eat and their aluminum moto-man, Jarvis, entered the room on whirring mechanical wheels. They'd named the artificial humanoid after one of Milly's favorite fictional characters.

"Is everything peachy here, sir?" Jarvis asked, in a voice that sounded like a stone stuck in the kitchen waste-compactor.

"Couldn't be better, Jarvis," Charlie quipped and Milly giggled.

"If that's all, sir, I shall retire for the night," the moto-man growled. "I'm feeling a tad puny."

Charlie and Milly watched in amusement as the metal creature whirred and crashed his way into the wall, backed up and went the opposite direction, backwards. Charlie shook his head. "He needs a bit of tweaking." Sparkles the dog followed after him, nipping at his wheels, his metal jaws chomping up and down.

Milly laughed and nodded. "I'll make sure they're both on idle before bedtime. They did make interesting conversation while you were gone, though."

"Oh, is that so?" Charlie asked.

Milly nodded. "Yes indeed! Jarvis learned three new words while you were away. He uses 'puny' quite a bit now."

After dinner, Jarvis loaded the dishes into the electric washer and Milly started into the living room to read. She glanced at Charlie. "We have things to discuss, mister, before you get too involved with your plants." Her eyes sparkled and Charlie nodded.

"Give me a few minutes, will you?"

She smiled mysteriously. "Go check on your plants. This can wait until you've had a good sleep. We'll talk at breakfast."

Charlie went to the library and flipped through his mail. Just as Milly mentioned, one letter was from the Olde-Fashioned Seed Company sent air-mail from Germany. He opened it and frowned as he scanned the letterhead. The address inside read "Applied Chemi-Culture, a Subsidiary of Olde-Fashioned Seed Company." The seed company was an established firm he'd ordered from many times. But now they owned Applied Chemi-Culture? He'd have to look into that. He couldn't remember the seed company changing ownership or merging with a hydro-ponics supply company. Charlie frowned as he read the letter. It seemed that there had been some cross-contamination in the last batch of seeds he'd ordered. They assured him that they'd replace the faulty seeds with a new shipment as soon as possible. Also, some sample seeds they meant to send him had been mixed up with an order to another lab. They enclosed a set of new seeds with their apologies for the slight mix-up.

Charlie shrugged and decided not to worry about it. There was probably an issue with the germination rate. It happened and it wasn't especially a problem for him since he used an electric germinator in both labs. So what if they'd had a "slight mix-up" in their samples? They claimed that they'd resolved the issue and that was good enough for him. Their samples were guaranteed. After all, it wasn't like he was trying to make medicine to save lives; he was simply growing a few tomatoes for his family. The fruit looked and tasted fine. Not just fine—it tasted great.

Charlie allowed himself one fast peek into the garden to satisfy himself that everything was all right then he went up to bed. Milly was already fast asleep. He quietly kissed her forehead, then climbed in, pressed the bedside button to increase the temperature of his blanket and fell into a deep sleep.

As Jarvis clattered around, setting the table for breakfast the next morning, Milly looked on, cringing as he flung china plates on the table. Maybe it was time to replace them with new plastic designs. She finally sat down and Charlie joined her. He gazed on the food with pride, realizing that all of the fruits and vegetables had been picked from his "home garden" chemi-culture system.

"I recognize that look in your eye, mister," she said. "It's the look of a man who provides well for his family."

"That I do!" he agreed, smiling as he watched his wife pick up a huge glass of bright red tomato juice and take a large gulp. The tomatoes had been grown in his "lab garden" and pulped, strained, seeded and juiced in the kitchen extractor.

"This is really good," she said, licking her lips. "Just the right mixture of tart and sweet with just a hint of salt."

Charlie beamed. "Not to mention highly nutritious and packed with vitamins as well."

She nodded slowly and grinned. "It's a good thing. Because the doctor says I need more vitamins."

Charlie stopped eating. "I knew you looked tired! Is everything all right?"

She nodded, her eyes sparkling. "Yes, everything's fine. But I'm afraid you'll have to expand the garden. It seems I'm eating tomatoes for two now."

Charlie dropped his fork and it clattered to his plate. "What?"

"You heard me, mister," she said, and her eyes danced as she took another gulp of the juice.

Charlie reached over and grabbed his wife's hand. Life was good. No—not just good; life was perfect. How could it not be, with all the things he'd accomplished and all the wonderful things they owned? And now this! Charlie's mind reeled. There would be one more person to feed in their family! He made a mental note to seed-out a few dozen more plants and make room in the greenhouse.

"Speechless, eh?" she said.

"Uh, yes, I am," Charlie admitted.

"Well, what do you have to say for yourself?" she teased.

"I'll have to order more seeds immediately!"

She laughed and shook her head, and they toasted each other with glasses of fresh tomato juice.

Charlie worked feverishly for the next few weeks in his home garden seeding and propagating new plants and ordered enough growing vats for a small greenhouse expansion. His time off was too short, and for the first time, he felt reluctant to go back to work. He suggested an extended leave, but Milly convinced him it was unnecessary. She assured him she'd be all right, and when she reminded him that his mother was close by to keep an eye on her, he finally relented.

"Promise you'll let me know if you need me?" he said.

She nodded and smiled. "We'll be fine here," she said, putting her hand on her stomach. "Your mother is keeping a close eye on us." Suddenly, she looked startled.

"Is everything all right?" he asked.

"Yes, I suppose. I could have sworn I felt the baby kick, but that's not likely at this point." She smiled. "Just first-time mother jitters."

"Probably just gas," Charlie said, laughing. "Maybe I should work on the acid-level in the tomatoes."

She swatted him and clutched him to her for another kiss, then pushed him towards the car. "How romantic you are, Charlie Rutherford. Now go back to work and leave me in peace to propagate."

He laughed. "Just call me Romeo," he teased, as he drove away.

Charlie felt displaced and uneasy the first few weeks back at work, but quickly got pulled into the politics and challenges of running the large laboratory. The "honeybee incident," as the lab workers called it, didn't seem to have any adverse effects on the resulting plants, and Charlie was able to produce twice as much as in previous years.

He kept himself busy over the next five months with his research and talked to Milly every night using the on-board communicator. In his time off, he swam in the large heated indoor pool, took long walks down the hallways of the ship and read in the massive library.

He was just planning an on-board educational conference on hydro-ponics for the staff and passengers when he got an urgent message from his mother. By the time he was finally able to speak to her, she was frantic.

"Charlie, honey, you need to get back down here to the hospital—fast! We have a problem. Milly's in the hospital!"

"Is she all right? Was she in an accident?" he clutched at his hair and paced the floor.

"Calm down, son. She's . . .well, there's no good way to say this. She's gone into labor! She's having the baby! It's too early and I'm so worried; can you come home?"

"I'll be home as soon as I can," he promised and clicked the communicator off.

He arranged for an emergency leave-of-absence and one of the on-board heli-plane pilots dropped him off right at the front doors of the hospital. He raced inside and found his mother pacing the floor in the waiting room.

"What happened?" he asked.

His mother shrugged. "Nothing, really. One minute she was fine, then the next she called me and said that she was having some pain. Apparently that mechanical monster of yours pressed the emergency alert buzzer and when it started beeping I knew something was really wrong. I hurried over to your house and found her passed out on the floor. The emergency service was alerted and brought her here. I can't believe she's in labor. It's too soon, Charlie! She has months to go before that baby is supposed to be born!"

"Right! There must be something else going on," Charlie said. "Have you talked to the doctor?"

She shook her head. "No, but the nurse told me that the baby was ready to be born—that it was full-grown already!"

They waited together for what seemed like hours. Soon, a distracted doctor in a white coat came into the waiting room. "Charlie Rutherford? Is there a Charles Rutherford here?" Charlie jumped up and said "That's me," and the doctor rushed over to him, shook Charlie's hand and clapped him on the back. "Congratulations, Charlie! You have a new baby boy."

Charlie glanced at this mother. "But doctor, it's too soon! They told my mother that the baby was full-grown! I don't understand what that means . . ."

The doctor nodded and smiled. "It means simply that the baby decided to be born, and he was born. Calm yourself! Your wife's fine, and the baby's fine, as far as we know."

"Really?"

The doctor nodded, then looked down at the floor. "There's just a slight abnormality, but I'm sure he'll grow out of it as he gets older. Trust me, it's nothing to worry about. We put him in the electric incubator just to be on the safe side but he didn't really need it."

Charlie swooned and the doctor led him to a chair. He slumped down into it. "Tell me the truth, doctor. What do you mean, abnormality? Is it because he was born early?"

The doctor frowned. "That's the crazy thing. It doesn't look like he WAS born early, like we thought. With all of our modern diagnosing devices, I usually don't get these kinds of things wrong. There must have been some miscalculation at the timing of conception. That's all idle speculation at this point. At any rate, your wife has delivered a full-term baby boy. Oddest thing; I just can't explain it. I'll take you to see him, but brace yourself."

Charlie swallowed and nodded. All sorts of horrors went through his mind—did the baby have enough toes and fingers? Was his brain normal? The doctor led him down the hall to the nursery and a couple of nurses stared at him, whispering, as he passed.

"I don't really know what to tell you," the doctor continued. "As far as we can tell, he's fine internally. It's just . .well, I'll let you see for yourself. We transferred him from the incubator ward to the nursery not long ago. The nurse will bring him to the window so you can take a peek."

Charlie was reluctant, but walked up to the window. The nurse picked up the baby and brought him closer. Charlie stared at his new son, swallowed and held his finger up to the window and gave it a little tap.

The doctor glanced at the baby then shrugged. "The coloring should even out as he gets more oxygen in his system."

The baby stared back with unfocused eyes and squirmed in his blue blanket. The nurse smiled, looked down at the infant then frowned.

The baby's head was bright, beet red. Charlie looked at the doctor, horror in his eyes.

The doctor smiled and nodded to the nurse, who moved closer to the window. "It's common for newborns to be flushed like this. Like I said, that will probably clear up after a while. I wouldn't be too concerned about that."

The baby flung his little fists out and squirmed and the blanket fell away from his head.

The baby's ears were bright, leafy green.

Charlie stared at the doctor and he shrugged. "So what'll you name him?" The doctor finally asked.

Charlie shook his head. "I . . . I'm not sure. I'll have to ask Milly."

The doctor nodded. "If you have any questions, don't hesitate to call and talk to the nurse." And with that, he hurried off down the hall, leaving Charlie with his own thoughts.

Charlie watched the baby for a while and when the nurse indicated that she was putting him back in the bed, Charlie made his way back to Milly's room.

He hugged and kissed her, but she was too tired to say much. "A name," she whispered. "We'll have to decide on a name."

Charlie nodded, trying to decide what to say. "Did you see him?" he finally asked.

Milly smiled and nodded. "Isn't he beautiful?"

Just then the nurse came bustling in and pushed him out of the room. "Your wife needs rest. You can come back for a visit tomorrow."

Charlie nodded, and reluctantly left the hospital and called a heli-cab to take him home. The nurse relented and let his mother sleep in a chair overnight to keep an eye on Milly. The house felt lonely and empty that night without Milly to keep him company. He sat down with Jarvis and Sparkles for a while and tried to play chess, but was too distracted. Jarvis always won, anyway. He finally ordered them both back into the corner and decreased power to idle mode.

He felt shivery and turned on the electric whole-house heater, then finally went to bed around midnight and fell into a fitful sleep. During the night, he dreamed about the Aristocrat Tomato Man and suddenly he was wide-awake. He hadn't thought about the Tomato Man for years—since he was a teenager.

Charlie's mind raced. He sat up in bed, thinking, a decision made. A grin slowly crept across his face. Before long, he started laughing. "Tom! His name will be Tom."

For a moment, he lay there thinking of all the possibilities then he jumped out of bed, pulled on his robe and ran to his garden. Now he knew what his next project would be.

He had a lot of work to do.

The popular view of Mars in the first half of the past century saw canals and Martians, an older race than ours, and mysterious in their ways. Burroughs, Heinlein, and others painted images of that world in passages made vivid through their evocative descriptions.

Mr. Bailey graduated from Cornell College in Mount Vernon, Iowa, where he studied English Literature and Religious Studies. Later this year he will take up residence at law school. Let's hope his legal pursuits do not keep him from writing more stories.

Meeting Across the River

By Michael McAndrews Bailey

The water in the Martian canal was as flat and smooth as a mirror. Cecily Eshleman walked through one of the many parks that lined the banks of the Deuteronilus Canal. Night had settled over Cherry Creek, and with it, an early winter cold. The lights lining the walking path flickered to life and Cecily saw her breath fogging in the air. Her entire body was sore and stiff. Basketball practice had been hell today—as it often was after a loss. The muscles in her thighs were still twitching and spasming.

Cecily hadn't changed back into her school uniform after practice, a violation of one regulation or another, but she didn't care. She rarely changed and she hadn't gotten into trouble yet. Her uniform was stuffed into her bag—Dad wouldn't like that, but she'd just hang it up in the bathroom in the morning and let the steam from her shower take care of any wrinkles. She was dressed instead in sweats over her practice uniform—they were baggy but warm. The hood of her sweatshirt was pulled up and she had the headphones of her tape player over her ears. It wasn't the shallow, jazzy pop her classmates listened to but the heavy, angsty, nostalgic bluestone tapes she'd stolen from Dad's collection.

The cold bit at Cecily's fingers as she pulled her hand out of her sweatshirt's pocket to massage her thigh muscles. The hellish practice had been entirely unfair punishment for her. She was a freshman, and while she was a budding star on the JV squad, she hardly saw the floor in varsity games unless they were blowouts. Last night's game had been close and Cecily could only watch from the bench as Cherry Creek had fallen to Sacred Heart 59-62.

Coach Amundsen was furious after losing such a close game. Practice today had been nothing but free throw drills and suicide sprints.

The trees that lined the path were narrow Martian maples that still had their bright red leaves despite the lateness of the season. They thinned out and Cecily could see the still waters of the Deuteronilus Canal that brought water from the Hellas Ocean east into the Tyrrhenum Wastes. Cherry Creek was spread out on the other side of the canal, while towards the west; she could just make out the distant lights of Second Nile.

Cecily was surprised to see a boat floating gently in the canal's water. Boats weren't unusual in the canal, but at this time of day and time of year, they were. Cecily came to a slow stop as she watched the boat pass by. Her breath caught in her throat. The boat was long and curving, and looked as if it had been grown, not made. It glittered with gold and jewels that were inlaid into calcified flesh, while banners streamed in the light wind. A dozen silhouetted figures were standing on the gondola. They were tall, slender and almost ethereal in their billowing robes and pastel hair.

Cecily forgot about her sore muscles and the practice from hell. The park was empty aside from the gondola and herself—there was no one else around to see it. She broke into a run, ignoring the pain in her legs as she pushed forward. A wide, white marble bridge spanned the entire width of the canal. She turned and run up the bridge just as the gondola was passing underneath. She leaned on the railing of the bridge and looked over. This wasn't the first time she'd seen the Balafar in person, but this was the closest she'd ever been to them and it was the first time she'd seen them this far from the walls of the Old City.

One of the Balafars looked up at Cecily. It looked like a young girl, but age and gender were always so hard to pick out with them. For a moment, their eyes met: Cecily's flat black and the Balafar girl's golden yellow. Cecily thought that maybe the corners of the girl's mouth turned up in a smile, but the gondola passed underneath the bridge. Cecily ran to the other side and looked over. The girl had turned and was staring back up at the bridge and Cecily. She waved, but the Balafar girl remained stoic as the boat disappeared into the night.

Cecily stood on the bridge for a few short while longer and watched after the boat until even its shape was gone in the darkness. She sighed and tried to start for home again, but her legs just wouldn't move. "Looks like this is my life now," she muttered.

She took a deep breath and filled her lungs with the cold, Martian air. The Balafar were aloof, ethereal and mysterious—seeing them out like this simply wasn't a thing anymore, not in the century and a half since first contact. But as the years and the centuries worn on, they become more and more rare, choosing instead to remain isolated and separate from the new world inside their crystalline cities.

She couldn't even remember the last time a Balafar had been seen out in public near Second Nile.

Cecily sighed again and managed to get her feet moving forward, finally making her way back home. Her house was just a few blocks off from the edge of the park. It was a large, gabled house with a green lawn in a nice neighborhood. Mommy wasn't back home yet—she was an engineer at one of the pump stations closer towards Second Nile—while Dad stayed at home during the day. He was a freelance writer, but Cecily wasn't entirely sure what that meant or what he did. Her oldest youngest brother, Merrick, sat in the front living room watching sports highlights on the evening news. He was only five months younger than Cecily, which she thought was awkwardly close, even for tube kids.

"You'll never guess what I saw today," Cecily said, pulling off her headphones.

Merrick only glanced up at Cecily out of the corner of his eyes. He was tall, lanky and was a member of his middle school's basketball team—but from what Cecily had heard from some of her younger friends who were still in middle school, he wasn't particularly good. "I heard you guys all had to run five miles today in practice," he said.

Cecily rolled her eyes. "Okay, it was only like two miles at most," she said. "But no, this happened on my way home." "What?"

"A Balafar gondola!"

Merrick raised an eyebrow "What?"

"You know, the weird elf people who live in those towers in the Old City," Cecily said.

"No, I know what the Balafar are, but a gondola?" "A boat you dorkus. A Balafar boat. In the canal!"

"So?"

"Do you know how often you see Balafars out and about?"

Merrick shrugged. "Who cares?"

"Whatever." Cecily sniffed the air. "Is Daddy making burritos?"

"It's Wednesday, so of course he is."

"Don't you take that tone with me, young man."

"Whatever," Merrick said, looking back at the television.

Cecily walked through the living room and into the dining room, where her three youngest siblings were doing their homework. Etta and Carolina were 10 and 9, and they were both struggling with their math—Etta with dividing fractions and Carolina with memorizing multiplication tables. Gideon was only five, so his homework was much simpler, repeatedly writing the words *we, my* and *like*.

"Hey guys." Cecily kissed each of them on the top of the head. "Math, huh?"

"Fractions are *dumb*," Etta said.

"Fractions are fun," Cecily said.

"That's because you're a nerd."

Cecily shrugged. "It's not going to get any easier from here on out." She was acutely aware of the discrete math homework burning a hole through her bag. "I wish I could go back to only dividing fractions."

"I don't have to do fractions," Gideon said.

Carolina had a forlorn look on her face. "I don't want to have to do fractions."

"Pretty much unavoidable but it won't kill you. It didn't kill me," Cecily said. "Or Merrick."

Cecily loved her brother, but he struggled in school and she was worried about the results he'd get on the PLAN test next semester. He likely wasn't going to wind up as one of those poor kids who got fry cook, but at the same time, he probably wasn't going to wind up being slotted into one of the more prestigious STEM fields like Cecily had—her school counselor was already talking about some of the top geography programs on Mars like Sojourner State Tipton.

She added, "I can help if you guys are stuck."

"Daddy says I have to try on my own first," Etta said.

That certainly sounded like him. "Don't get too stuck because supper's almost ready."

Etta and Carolina both nodded their heads and kept working. Dad friend something over the stove in the kitchen while Perry was busy washing dishes. Perry was an International Business Machine HouseBot 9600, with a wheeled base and a vaguely humanoid torso.

Its eyes were pale blue lights in its small head while its exterior was all white plastic and shiny chrome.

"Welcome home, Cecily," Perry said.

"Hey Perry," Cecily said. She stopped at the stove next to Dad. "Steak?"

Dad was browning small strips of steak in a frying pan, and there were covered pans of Mexican rice and black beans on the back of the stove. Cecily's mouth watered "Not just steak," Dad said. "Nilyig beef."

"Nilyig? Isn't that expensive?"

"It can be."

"Seems almost like a waste."

Dad shrugged. "I've got a few more steaks in the fridge for this weekend. Thinking of grilling some."

"Can I have two?" Cecily asked.

"Two what?" Dad asked.

"Two burritos," Cecily said. Dad's burritos were always large, but Cecily was starving.

"I dunno," Dad said. He glanced over at Perry. "Well, can she?"

"Cecily walked 4.12 miles to and from school today. While at school, she walked 0.94 miles. She spent 150 minutes at basketball practice, where she ran 2.54 miles and spent another 33 minutes lifting weights," Perry reported. "For breakfast, she had—"

"Get to the point, tin can," Dad said.

"Based on today's activities and caloric intake, Cecily could be allowed to have two burritos for supper tonight without violating standard caloric intakes."

Cecily grinned.

"There might not be leftovers," Dad said.

"There's always plenty of leftovers!" Cecily said.

"Fine, fine, you can have two," Dad said.

Cecily clapped her hands together. "Oh thank God, I was starving," she said. "But you'll never guess what I saw today."

"Oh?"

"A Balafar!"

Dad looked at her, surprised. "You don't say?"

"Not just one, but a dozen!"

"A dozen Balafars? You're joking."

"No I'm not! They were on a boat in the canal."

"What were they doing?" Dad asked.

Cecily shrugged. "I dunno. Whatever it is that Balafars do on boats in a canal. One of them even smiled at me."

"Balafars don't smile. They don't have human emotions."

"Well this one did," Cecily said stubbornly. "She was polite and cute and smiled at me!"

"*She* was cute?" Dad said, apparently more interested in the gender of the Balafar than the Balafars themselves.

Cecily felt her cheeks burn. "Shut up, dad," she said. "It's not like that. I don't even know if it was a girl or a boy or how old they are!"

"The Balafar are like that. I don't think anyone knows if they actually have sexes or gender or age," Dad said. He grabbed a fork and stabbed one of the slices of meat. He took a bite of it and nodded his head approvingly. "It's been a while since anyone's seen them outside of the Old City." While he spoke, he handed the fork to Cecily who chewed on the steak—it was soft and tender. Cecily wanted more, but she could wait. "We should tell someone about it."

Cecily shrugged. "I don't see why we should. They're technically sort of Americans so they can do as they want."

"Well aren't we just the sharpest lil' constitutional law attorney this side of D.C."

Cecily jabbed her father in the arm with the fork's tines.

"Get changed. Supper's almost ready," Dad said.

It was morning, and Cecily was getting dressed to go shopping. The dress she chose was a confirmation gift from last year, and she was surprised that it still fit her—though the hemline was a bit higher on her thighs and the top felt tighter around her chest and shoulders. She would to ask Dad if he could loosen it up—she thought the length was fine. She'd added about two inches to her height and a good 10, 15 pounds since her confirmation—some of it was from muscle and some of it from having grown—Perry had assured her of that. She pulled on leather boots over black leggings and zipped them up. When she was done, she stood up, smoothed out her skirt and left her bedroom.

Etta, Carolina and Gideon sat on the couch in the living room watching the tail end of their Saturday morning cartoons while Mom was sitting in her favorite chair reading a copy of *Time*. Cecily looked at her siblings and then at Mom. "Where's Dad?" she asked. "And Merrick?"

Mom didn't answer, and Cecily worried that she'd maybe stepped on a potentially hazardous landmine. She glanced down at the three of them on the couch. They were focused on the cartoon and weren't paying Mom or Cecily any attention.

Mom cleared her throat and said, "They're coming."

Cecily nodded her head and didn't push the matter—the tone in Mom's voice was enough to tell her not to. She'd thought that she'd heard Merrick come home late last night—again—so he was probably getting a long lecture from Dad. Cecily sat down on the edge of the couch and watched as the three animated dogs tried to find a way to get off the small island they were stranded on.

Dad and Merrick came into the room not long after Cecily sat down. Dad had his near-constant sardonic smile on his face, while Merrick was sulking as usual. Mom looked up from her magazine and asked, "Ready?"

"Ready as we'll ever be," Dad said.

"Let's go then," Mom said, standing up. Etta stood up, walked over to the TV and turned it off. Gideon seemed upset, but Cecily grabbed his hand and gave it a light squeeze.

"I've seen this one," Cecily lied. "I can tell you how it ends."

Gideon thought about it and shrugged. "Perry will record it for me. I can watch later."

"Okay then," Cecily said.

The seven of them left the house, turning off all the lights and leaving Perry in his charging station in the kitchen—his small vacuum cleaner drones would scrub the house while they were gone. Even though Cecily was the oldest, she sat in the back of the Ford station with Gideon. He had a small pile of books in the back that he'd read on car trips—often to Cecily—though the drive into Second Nile wasn't long. The books were still simple things with large fonts and large pictures, but they were still more complex than what Cecily could remember reading at his age.

Merrick, Etta and Carolina sat in the middle row, while Mom drove and Daddy fiddled with the radio in the front. Etta and Carolina talked quietly to each other about some television show they both watched but Cecily had never heard of before—making her feel old and slightly out of it at 14—and Merrick stared absently out the car window.

Cecily shook her head and turned her attention back to Gideon reading one of his new books, a small one called *Down from the Attic*. He read slowly with his finger moving across the page with each word. If he came across a word he didn't know, Cecily would let him stumble over it to see if he could get it himself before helping him out. If he was able to get through a word himself without her help, she would clap her hands together and congratulate him on it. He beamed with pride each time, and even once told her to be quiet while he was trying to sound out a word on his own.

Mom left Cherry Creek behind and exited onto the Interstate that ran parallel with the Deuteronilus Canal and would take them into Second Nile. She switched over from manual and let the car's computer take over driving after she merged into traffic on the Interstate. Mom could have turned on the autodriver before leaving, but it was often clumsy in the suburban residential streets and was far better suited for Interstate driving—but Cecily wasn't entirely sure if she trusted a computer over a dozen miles away beaming instructions to the car was good substitute for a human driver.

Second Nile was a sprawling mass of stepped pyramid-like sky-scrapers rising thousands of feet into the air, and many of them had skywalks and skyways connecting them—a few of them even had tunnels running right through them for the elevated skyways. Cecily felt her stomach turn over as the Interstate passed through a valley between several of the towering skyscrapers. She kept her eyes down and helped Gideon finish the book, but the sense of vertigo didn't go away entirely.

Beyond the new city center was the Old City; it was a clutch of tall and narrow crystalline towers that were mostly abandoned. Second Nile had once been an important Balafar city thousands of years ago, but it had slowly crumbled as the planet dried up and birth rates plummeted. The American city of Second Nile had been built around the ancient Balafar city, while the few remaining Martians closed themselves off in their towers.

At the edge of the old city was an ancient curtain wall that had once protected the Old City, but was now only a crumbling relic and a tourist attraction. An outdoor bazaar had once sat at the base of the wall, but over time, it had been replaced by a more modern outdoor shopping center. Some of the Balafars who lived in the Old City could sometimes be found roaming the Old City Outdoor Shopping Center like the relics of the long-passed age that they were—but most people hardly payed any attention to them.

Mom took over control of driving when the car got off at the shopping center's exit. It was an early Saturday morning and the shopping center was packed, but somehow Mom was able to find parking. "Stay close, children," she said as everyone got out of the car.

Cecily held onto Gideon's hand as they made their way through the crowd. They had to deal with not only other pedestrians, but also with cars trying to pull in or pull out. Since Gideon was five and didn't fully grasp the concept of how dangerous cars could be, Cecily had to hold him tight to keep him from bouncing off and into danger. She thought she had a firm grip on his hand, but she heard him gasp and then his hand slipped free of hers.

"Gideon!" she cried out, but he had already disappeared into the crowd. She heard someone—probably Mom—call out her name, but she ignored her. "Gideon! Gideon Eshleman!"

Cecily pushed against the flow of the crowd, desperately trying to find her brother. She heard screams and shouts; her heart leapt into her throat and she broke into a run, following the screams. She saw pastel-colored hair over the tops of the crowd. Her heart was beating faster as she broke through the crowd. Five Balafars stood before her and a sixth that was rising from the ground. Gideon had fallen onto his rear in the collision and was on the verge of tears—almost nobody took notice of the Balafar; people gave them plenty of room but none of their attention.

"Gideon!" Cecily cried out and ran to her brother. She knelt down next to him and wiped his eyes and nose with the sleeve of her sweater.

A firm voice shouted something at her, and it took her a few moments to register the words as Laconic Martian. She looked up and saw a Balafar male standing over her. He was tall, thin and impossibly beautiful. The gold circlet he wore in his soft green hair glittered in the dim sunlight; the he wore robes were thick and willowy, with gold and silver lace sown into it. The other Balafars behind him were dressed similarly and looked similar to him. A family.

"Are you this creature's mother?" the Balafar demanded in Martian. *"We demand recompense for his transgression."*

Cecily put her arms around Gideon and hugged him. *"Don't you lay a finger on him,"* she hissed in Laconic Martian.

The Balafar was taken aback; although he'd been making his threats and demands in Martian, he hadn't expected Cecily to under- stand him, hadn't excepted her to respond back and he certainly hadn't been expecting her to be so defiant. It took him a few moments to compose himself before he said, *"You dare speak to me that way, you insolent urchin?"*

"Insolent urchin?" Cecily repeated. This could get bad, but she didn't see an easy way out of it. A small crowd was beginning to gather, but none of them seemed interested in helping. *"Maybe if you—"*

A figure stepped forward and put itself between Cecily and the Balafar. It took her a few seconds to realize it was another Balafar—a smaller, younger one. The younger one began to speak to the older one; their conversation was in a more archaic, formal form of Martian that moved too fast for Cecily. Gideon cried into her chest. She rubbed the back of his head and made soft noises to calm him down. The conversation came to an end after a tense minute; the older Balafar turned around, said something to the group and retreated.

The younger Balafar turned around to face Cecily. She—Cecily assumed it was a girl by the slight bust hidden underneath her robes— was smiling lightly. "Hello," she said, her accent dropping the h and shifting the e slightly. Her eyes were yellow-gold, and her hair light pink. "Are you hurt?"

Cecily couldn't speak. She only shook her head.

"Father can be… not nice sometimes," the girl said. She bowed at the waist. *"For these crimes, I apologize on behalf of my clan,"* she said in Laconic Martian.

Cecily gaped at the girl and realized she had to say something. *"Apology accepted."*

The Balafar girl stood smoothed out her robes and smiled again at Cecily before turning around and following after her family. It was only then that Cecily realized that she had been the same girl she'd seen the other day.

"Cecily?"

Cecily looked over her shoulder and saw her parents standing at the edge of the crowd.

"What… what was that?" Mom asked.

Cecily shrugged. "I don't know," she said. She looked after the Balafars but they were gone. "I honestly have no idea."

Here's a story that harkens back to pulp fiction detectives of the thirties and forties, where protagonists are hard-bitten, women mysterious, and there's no problem that a good shot of bourbon won't fix.

Mr. Mantle lives in Vancouver, where he writes fantasy and science fiction.

The Coil

By Sebastien Mantle

It always starts out the same, with the light. Through a haze I look ahead to the luminescent wall searing my retinas. And I feel a cold beyond the clammy chill of my soaked through coat. That coldness, it has something to do with the slender speck of shadow at the base of the wall of light, growing and shrinking with the pulsations of the swirling brightness. I cry out with a hoarse voice for the shadow to stop, to get away from the light.

It turns around, and for an instant I can see the glazed eyes of a young girl staring from a gaunt face. She's smiling at me, and that smile freezes my blood. I reach out, but I know it's too late. There's too much distance between us. She turns her brilliant smile towards the light, and reaches to touch it…

I wake with a strangled shout, my chest tight. Sitting up, I clutch my sweat drenched forehead, trying not to think about the dream. The memory. Avoidance, it's a morning ritual to me these days. Beams of sunlight filter through my knockoff bamboo curtains. Eventually, the cold sweat stops and I get up to tread from my bed to my bathroom. After a shower, I pour a tumbler full of bourbon from a bottle on the kitchen counter. The cheap stuff.

When you choke down as much as I do, you stop caring about the taste. Wailing sirens and whistles of steam engines mingle outside into a chaotic cacophony of sound. I down my drink, pour another, and go to my window. A zeppelin casts its shadow several meters up as it glides lazily through the sky above the sprawling city, and I watch it glide through sinuous clouds of steam, and smoke rising from the streets below. Sunlight gleams off the speeding monorail on its zigzagging way through the city, taking commuters high up above the ground to zip along between skyscrapers, trailing white steam behind it.

But even as I try to notice everything else, in the center of it all, is the Coil. A spiraling tube of pulsating light trapped within a fortified glass and copper encasement, rising so far above the skyline its tip touches the clouds. They call it the future, a device that can wirelessly transfer infinite amounts of energy, anywhere. Free and limitless electricity. A huge glowing super conductor, right in the middle of one of the most densely crowded cities in the world.

I lift my glass to my mouth and drain it, letting burning alcohol sooth away some of the tension knotting my stomach. I go to the door, unlatch it, and blindly grab the rolled up newspaper I know is waiting for me. Taking it to my armchair, a battered old thing upholstered in black leather in a dark corner of the room, I throw myself onto the worn cushion. I click on my lamp, cordless like all CoilTech technology, and flip through the paper. It's the usual Manhattan garbage. Political scandals, proposals for civic planning in the inner city, the closing of a famous pancake diner.

I almost flip past it, but something in an article catches my eye. The headline reads: "Missing son of Jewel tycoon found dead."

Michael Brant, only son of Hugh Brant, owner of the biggest diamond distributor in the state. The nineteen year old went missing six months ago. I scan the paragraph. Found in an alley across town, cause of death unclear, but possibly heart trauma. There it is, the part that caught my eye. "Strange burn mark across palm of left hand." It could be a coincidence, hell, it most likely is. "The cause of the injuries is unclear, as is the identity and motive of the killer." It was assumed at first that the boy ran off. But if so, he didn't take anything with him. No clothes, no money. When a month went by the reward money started being offered, the search parties organized. Two months, no word. Three months, four…

They called it a possible kidnapping, but there was never any ransom demand. "Odd," I muse out loud.

The phone rings. I ignore it at first. Most calls I get these days are bill collectors, and the odd person who wants a job done. Always the same jobs, typical low level detective work. They call me because of my reputation from my days in the force, and I turn them down every time. This time, after about the twelfth ring, I start to wonder if they'll give up. After the twentieth I give up. Slapping my newspaper down atop a precarious pile, I cross the room and lift the receiver to my mouth. "'Lo?"

"Mr. Drake?" The voice is British and professionally dry.

"Who's asking?" I've already figured this is a collection agency, but I've gone and answered the phone, might as well know before I hang up on this shmuck.

"Detective Ethan Drake?"

I haven't been a detective in ten years. Would a debt collector call me by that modifier? "Yes, yes, now what do you want?"

"Mr. Drake, this is Mr. Weston, calling from IES. We were referred to you specifically. We hope that you can help us in regards to a… delicate situation that we have."

IES—Integrated Energy Systems. The parent company of CoilTech. IES invented and owns the Coil, making them the most powerful organization in the state. This day isn't starting out good.

"Sorry, can't help you,' I say despite my burning curiosity. The biggest emerging energy company in the world, calling a retired street cop. This had to be something big. No. I move the receiver from my ear, determined to slam it down and walk away.

"A Ms Ezla gave me your name, sir; she was very adamant that we call you, and only you."

As soon as I hear the name, I'm glued to the receiver. Good or not, today was certainly not starting out boring. I can't let off how curious I am, though. I want him to have to work to convince me, let slip as much as possible before I make a decision. "Well, I'm not sure what she told you, but I'm retired, have been for a long time."

"So I've been led to understand, Detective Drake. But we were hoping you'd consult with us on this one matter."

"Look, buddy. For one, you can drop the detective crap, I quit. Two, I don't even know what this is about yet. I'm not about to drag my ass across town in rush hour traffic to find out I'm being called in to bust some kid for graffiti. I'm a busy man, so make this quick." That last part's a lie, but this chump doesn't need to know that. Neither does Lin Ezla, for that matter. How many years has it been? Eight, nine since we last talked? I don't regret it anymore per se; enough time goes by and you stop self-pitying over the past. Still, it's got my interest piqued.

"Well we've had some... I'll just call them breaches in our security for now. It's raised some safety concerns."

"Alright, but why call me?"

"We are also under a small degree of pressure from the mayor's office to resolve the issue, rather than have the public police force spend resources."

It's one perk about owning virtually all the electricity in the city. Since all police vehicles and weapons, as well as the energy for government facilities, switched to CoilTech technology, IES is allowed to run their own internal investigations when it comes to possible criminal activity on their property to preserve company secrets, and maintain the structural integrity of the ever so precious machine. What I'm getting from this dust cloud's wording is that something big's gone down, something that the police are itching to get their paws into.

"What kind of security breaches?" I'll keep baiting the bastard, even though I know I'm not getting anything too specific, not over the phone. Something's going on that IES wants to keep very quiet.

"Mr. Drake, if you could just come by, we'll brief you the full details. We could really use your help."

"And what do I get out of helping you?"

"The company is willing to compensate you substantially for the trouble, if you can help us solve our issue. The starting offer I've been told to quote to you is one hundred thousand in international credits."

International credits, currency that maintains minimum value no matter what country you're in. And in economies where the dollar is low, it'll average out to an equivalent worth, in countries where the dollar is high, international units still maintain the value of whatever country they're issued from. That kind of cash can go a long way, worldwide. Whatever this situation of theirs is, it's bad. "Sorry, no can do, not without some idea of what I'm looking at."

"Sir, please."

"Bye," I slowly move the receiver away.

"There's been a death."

I pause. "What kind of death?"

"If you'd just come down to IES—"

"A death in the CoilTech facility?!" I'm not even trying to hide my interest now.

"Y—yes."

"I'll be there in an hour." I slam the receiver down. From my bedside drawer I pull out my pistol in its worn leather holster where its been for years, untouched except for a semi annual cleaning. Even when I was in the force the weapon pushed the line of legality. All police weaponry had switched to CoilTech tasers, and lethal force has long been outlawed. The stainless steel revolver is an antique. I only get away with it because of its custom ammunition. Right now I have it loaded with three basic rubber bullets, a stick charge gel taser, a tracker, and an expanding foam unit. I just don't feel like I'm at work without it by my side.

The train rattles and shakes under my feet. I'm a broke bastard, no mistake, but not so broke that I need to use public trains to get around. There's an old beat up car in the parkade of my building, hell, it's even running on a CoilTech energy receiver. But trains help me think.

To this day, CoilTech either hasn't perfected a train engine on Coil power, or they haven't managed to buy out the contracts from the companies still producing old school steam engines. It isn't far in the coming, though. CoilTech may not have its claws in the engineering side of public transport, but it managed over two decades ago to get all trains running on its software. Everything from guidance systems to temperature control, very little in this city remains that isn't dependent on CoilTech. And the ground is shrinking under anyone trying to resist progress.

The train is silent but for an occasional cough or sleepy mumble. I stand with one hand on the overhead railing, my hat pulled down low to shade my eyes from harsh lights above.

A TV screen mounted on the far wall of the train car flickers with black and white images from behind scribbled graffiti, as a female reporter gives the latest news on Iran, recently joining the swell of nations to sign contracts with the U.S in exchange for the promise of CoilTech. Where our government ends and IES begins is becoming less and less clear to me. It's like the world is up for sale, and CoilTech is the universal price. I turn my attention to the window, and see the Coil, like a massive glowing centerpiece to the city, disappearing into the grey clouds that overcast the sky.

Of course, it all hinges on good old New York. We're the first, and so far, the only city to use IES technology as a main power source. Legal issues prevented IES from releasing CoilTech to the world without a testing period of fifty years. So they went big, using one of the most densely populated cities in the world to prove just how safe and reliable the Coil is. At the end of this year, the testing period is up. Just a few months before every major city on earth sports its own big glowing bug zapper.

That thought didn't always leave such a bad taste in my mouth. I'm pushing forty, which means I've spent my entire life in a city with Coil energy at the forefront. By the time I joined the force in my twenties, everything from weapons to radios to vacuum cleaners were powered via remote energy from the glowing tower. "A utopia of clean and limitless energy." I heard and read those words so often, saw the speeches and slogans growing up, that for most of my life I've taken for granted that this technology really would bring us to a brighter future.

Ten years ago I was made to doubt that, and now, I see Utopia rotting from the inside. With the steady advance of CoilTech into multiple facets of industry, factories as well as toll booths and other service stations are automated. Unless you own shares in the company, work for them, were born into money or are lucky enough to have held onto one of the dwindling jobs left, you're screwed. "Limitless, free energy." Except free is a misnomer. The fuel cells sold to other nations from the excess power of the Coil make the government and IES a tidy profit, along with payoffs from partnering nations chomping at the bit for the revolutionary technology. It helped us out of the depression, but in these streets, I've seen neighborhoods where you'd think the depression never ended.

I brood as the train speeds through tunnels and over bridges, the view from the window an indistinct blur of grey stone, save for one constant, the Coil, glowing bright in the center as if it were the sun and Manhattan its solar system. This is already the closest I've been to the damn thing in ten years. I can't deny feeling like there's some sort of unfinished business there. A feeling like I should revisit that place where I lost faith in my career and let my life go to hell. It's a feeling I've been good at ignoring. Until now.

I step off the train onto a grimy platform. Already I feel a slight electric tingle, like static, making the hairs on my arms and neck stand up. Experts insist this feeling is purely psychological, that the Coil's energy is both invisible and intangible until it connects with one of its receivers. Paranoid shmuck that I may be, even I am willing to admit that maybe it's all in my head.

I avoid looking at the light as I descend the stairs out of the station. Instead I focus on following a haphazard trail of people walking to the double door entrance to IES, the circular structure that forms a ten-story wall around the Coil. The doors slide open to reveal a small lobby with white walls and not much else. People stand in line up in front of a large grey metal door at the other end of the room, scanning keycards on a small glowing window one by one and stepping through when the door opens. I idly wonder what happens if someone tries to sneak in behind an employee without his or her own access card.

I turn my attention to a small service window to the side, with a sign above it that reads "Visitor registration." A square faced woman sits on the other side amid a cloud of cigarette smoke, reading a magazine. No automated greeting machine for IES headquarters, I suppose. I step over and tap the counter. The hag puts the rag down with an exaggerated sigh and croaks through the intercom: "Good morning, and welcome to IES; how may I help you today?"

"Drake, I'm expected." I wait while she sifts through pages in a massive logbook. A gaudily painted fingernail slides down a page. She nods before sliding it across to me through the opening in the window. "Sign here, and mark the time. Right now it's—"

"I got it," I fish out my pocket watch, a large piece made of tarnished brass on a brass chain, older than the Coil, older than me. Analog watches and clocks are a thing of the past, replaced by CoilTech digital timepieces. I like things old fashioned. I write the time down next to my name, which is already written down in a professionally neat hand. "So which way do I go?"

"Detective Drake?"

I spin around faster than I can think at the unexpected voice from behind, my hand reaching within my coat to grasp the worn handle of my revolver. I stop halfway to pulling the weapon free. The man in front of me is in his late fifties, with short-cropped grey hair that's balding in the front. Dark eyes peer out from a wrinkled face behind small round spectacles. "Detective? It's Weston, we talked earlier," same British voice. He holds out a hand to shake mine.

Slowly, I let go of my holstered weapon. "It's Ethan, or Mr. Drake if you insist on being formal. Not detective, not anymore."

Weston nods with a polite smile. A section of wall is missing, presumably where a sliding door was installed to look like part of the lobby wall, right next to the service window. The hag must have pressed a button somewhere. "Were you waiting in there for me all damn morning?"

Another polite smile. "You are a very important guest today Detec—Mr. Drake. There is much to discuss, please follow me." Weston turns and walks into the secret doorway, and, slowly, I follow. Within is a tiny room with what looks like an elevator at the other end. A small metal table is positioned to the right, with an IES security guard behind it.

"If you'd please leave any and all weapons here, then we can proceed."

My whole body tenses. "Not happening," my voice is almost a growl.

"Mr. Drake, I'm afraid it's company policy for your safety as much as ours."

"You can shove your protocol; you don't call in a cop and then take his gun at the door, that's not how this works, bud."

Mr. Weston retains his calm, if with a bit of coolness. "If I recall you were quite insistent on saying you are retired. All guests here, regardless of job or station, go by the same rules."

"Then you can forget my helping you. No one's getting my piece, end of story."

After a few tense moments, Weston nods. "Very well." He presses a button and the elevator doors slide open. "This way."

The ride down is longer than I expected. Not surprisingly, IES is a larger facility than it appears. When the doors open, I'm faced with a long grey walled hallway with a lime green linoleum floor, lit by harsh fluorescents. Our footsteps echo down the hall. Near the end, Mr. Weston turns to a door on the left and opens it, stepping aside with a gesture for me to go in first. Patting the holstered gun under my coat for reassurance, I step in. The dark room flickers to light, and I involuntarily gasp. My breath mists in front of me in a refrigerated room. On metal slabs in neat rows, lay at least two dozen corpses. *What the hell have I got myself into...*

"You're earlier than expected, for a change," comes a crisp female voice. I turn, and I'm face to face with Lin Ezla. My ex wife. She walks into the room, black high heels clacking rhythmically on the floor, brunette curls bouncing with each step. And abruptly I'm being held in a tight hug, feeling the contours of her lithe, muscular body pressed against me. With a kiss on the cheek she breaks the hug, caressing the side of my face with a cool, slender hand. "You need a shave, and you've lost too much weight." Her smile is warm, and stunning. "I've missed you."

For a moment a half strangled grunt is all I can get out. I almost forget the cadavers filling the chilled room. When I remember, I shiver. "Lin, what the hell is going on here? I was told of *a* death, not twenty. This is big, too big even for your bosses to keep under wraps."

"Which is exactly why I gave them your name. If you can figure this out, stop this from happening again, we can try to avoid this going public. IES can move forward in the new year as a worldwide sustainable energy source. I know that's not necessarily what you want,' she continues in a gentle tone. "But you're the best man for the job. You'll have all the credits you need, and maybe even answers. Peace of mind, a chance to leave the past behind you where it belongs."

Answers, she's got me there. A hook better than money, or her looks. Answers to a decade old question that's haunted me. If I can find out what happened back then, I can expose IES. Such a young girl, dead, and these bastards covered it up, pressured my bosses to keep it hushed. "What if I refuse, here and now, and walk away, seeing what I've seen?"

Lin shakes her head ruefully, biting her lip in that way I remember. "Ethan, my dear, who would believe you now? You're not exactly the most credible witness."

She's right, alcoholic ex cop vs. IES, I wouldn't have a leg to stand on.

"Here," Lin pulls a thick manila file from her handbag and hands it to me. "Look through this." The woman knows I've made up my mind. I'm taking the case. I start walking between bodies as I flip through the sheets. Photos, reports, missing person posters. I glance from photos to cadavers and back. The victims are all over the spectrum, from barely adolescent teens to middle aged men and women; from well to do business people to homeless addicts. Black and white and in between. My breath mists before me as I pace through the macabre freezer. Mr. Weston and Lin silently watch. The deceased have but one common feature. Marks, like burns or bruises, spiraling on their left forearms and marring their palms. And, when I turn a body over, using my coat sleeves as gloves, I find a spot on the back of the neck to match.

I speak so abruptly that I see Lin almost jump, but I see her from the corner of my eye as I continue to stare at the stiff in front of me. "So when you found the Brant kid dead, who's idea was it to dump him in an alley?" Weston's gasp turns into a cough. I turn and look first Weston, then Lin, in the eyes. "Is this the promising career you wanted? I'm surprised your bosses didn't just hide his death like they did these bastards, or could Hugh Brant not be bought off?"

Weston stammers in protest, but I keep my gaze intent on Lin. His voice might as well be TV static in the background.

Lin's reply is so cool and detached, I start to wonder if I even know who she is anymore. "Hugh Brant and his wife agreed to silence, under the condition that their son's body be made available to them for burial."

Suddenly, the part of this whole thing that confused me the most is the only part that makes sense. It would be ludicrous to dump one particular body where it could be found, while keeping the rest hidden. Unless the victim's family had some way of knowing, or at least suspecting, the company's involvement. And obviously they couldn't miraculously produce the corpse of their missing son, explaining the way in which the corpse was allowed to be found. "But why? Why would they be willing to stay quiet? This can't be legal, even for you people."

"There's no foul play here, Ethan, and any legal liabilities are ours to deal with, and will not affect you. I promise."

I sigh. "Suicide again, right? Don't give me that crap, Lin. There's more to this and I think you know it. Besides, even if IES is allowed its own internal investigations department it doesn't make it legal for you to dump bodies out in the city." I realize I'm clenching my fist on the file, crumpling it. "How? How was this allowed to happen again? I thought security was doubled, after what happened to the girl."

"These people… We believe they're operating as a group, a suicide cult of some sort. It's always one at a time, every week—"

"Jesus, Lin! How long have you been keeping these stiffs frozen here?"

Lin steps closer, and lowers her voice. "Ethan, my employers want you to do one thing, and one thing only, and that's to track this group, and report their location, to prevent this from continuing. That's it, that's all."

"So much for my answers," I mutter with a sneer I can't suppress.

She shakes her head almost imperceptibly, her eyes flickering to the right, indicating Mr. Weston a few feet behind her shoulder. That warning look in her eyes means be quiet.

I take the file with me when I leave. There's so much buzzing through my head, so many pieces that I know fit together, just not how. So I start from what I do know.

I drive uptown to the Brant estate, a monolith of antique red brick and statuesque marble work, with intricate fountains and bush sculptures dotting the massive front yard. I park half a block up, and walk my way back to the house. It's fenced off behind thick iron bars, of course. I work my way around to the back, careful to stay behind neat trees and bushes, careful not to be seen by the guard sitting in the booth at the double gate.

find the service entrance in the back, a small single door leading out to an equally small gate, for trash to be brought out and supplies brought in. The estate sits on a rare bit of land not overrun with crowded together buildings, sporting a small copse of trees behind it. I squat down against a tree and wait.

While I do this, I go through the file more, looking for connections. A death a week, all on Sunday nights, all around the same time, between midnight and 2 a.m. I notice something else. While the older victim's are from all across the social and financial spectrum-in fact mostly being between lower and middle class- the younger ones all share a commonality: every one of them comes from a family of affluent wealth, and/or from a family with business connections to IES. It could be nothing, but it brings me to question the suicide cult theory. If senior members were recruiting young rich kids, they certainly wouldn't be going to meet their makers before the young rich kids. It makes no sense, people who recruit others into these kinds of things either want to die with them en masse, or right after, or not at all. It just doesn't fit.

Iron creaks against iron, and I jump to my feet. One of the cleaning staff is bringing bags out to a locked metal dumpster leaning on the fence. Carefully, I step out of the shadow of the trees as the aproned woman fumbles with the lock. Moving as quickly and silently as I can, I slip through the service gate and through the door.

I pass the kitchen and laundry rooms, through a nondescript door and into the house itself, lavishly decorated, with a floor of shining marble and a spiraling staircase of polished oak. I ignore the paintings and statues, and dash upstairs, hoping I don't get spotted. I feel my blood pumping hot through my veins. The thrill of the chase, I haven't felt it in ages, and I can't deny to myself that it feels good.

Carefully, I peek into rooms. An office, a lounge. Finally, I find what I think I'm looking for. A bedroom, lavish but too small to be the master suite, with sports trophies and posters of models decorating the walls. I step in. When the maid straightens up from where she'd been bent over dusting, I freeze at the same time as she does. We stand, silently, and I think my eyes must be almost as wide as hers. "Policia," I say softly, raising a hand. Her eyes go wider if anything, and shift around as if looking for others. "I… I'm no supposed to talk to you. You can't be here."

"I'll make it quick, it's important. I need to know what you can tell me about Michael, what was he like, before he disappeared?"

"I no supposed to say." She looks scared.

I sigh, and pull out a small stack of bills I brought. *One hundred thousand international credits,* I remind myself as I hold out the money. The maid cranes her neck to peer over my shoulder, then quickly snatches the bills. "He acted strange, not right."

"What do you mean?"

"He stayed in room, and when he came out, he spoke very little. And… " she hesitates.

"And what?"

"Things started to happen around him. Bad things. Dog dead, glass breaking without being touched, power on and off. I was… I was scared of him."

"Did he ever mention anything out of the ordinary? Anything new that may have happened to him?"

She shakes her head frantically.

"Are you sure?"

She nods.

"Ok. Go, continue your work. I'm going to look around the room for a minute, then I'll see myself out." She walks out at something close to a run, and I close the door gently behind her. I need to do this quickly, there's no telling if the petty cash I gave the maid will buy her silence. I open drawers in the massive oak dresser, rifling through clothes. Nothing. I check the closet, I check the nightstand and under the bed. My questing fingers feel under the mattress and touch on something. The book I pull out is a small leather journal. I flip it open to a random page. The handwriting is all over the place, completely erratic:

The defective one will free us.

The defective one will free us.

The defective one will free us.

It's the same message, over and over, page after page, scrawled in massive letters and jotted in small ones throughout the journal. I can't make heads or tails of it.

I'm almost too distracted by the journal to take note of the sound of boots in the hallway, but when I realize what I'm hearing, I curse under my breath. The maid must have gone straight to security. I stride over to the window and fling it open. There's a two story drop below, but decorative vines climb up the wall. The doorknob behind me turns. I swing myself out and grab hold of the vines just as the guard yells inside the room. I climb down halfway before my foot slips, and my weight tears the vines down. I fall the rest of the way to land on my back, the air in my lungs bursting out in a heavy grunt of pain.

An alarm sounds. I rise to my feet and hobble across the lawn, back to the service gate. A guard is in my way, running towards me, drawing his taser. In one smooth motion I draw my pistol and fire. The shock round hits him and he goes down, unconscious. I get out of the gate and start running. My legs feel like they're on fire by the time I stop to catch my breath. I take on a neutral pace when I reach the roac, walking as if I don't have a care in the world. The journal is tucked safely in my coat pocket, whatever good it'll do me.

<hr>

Bourbon helps numb my bruised back, but it doesn't do much for my thoughts. I'm back at my apartment, staring blankly at the open journal on my table as I swig liquor right out of the bottle. Not a single address, not a single number, no personal revelations, no clues. The book has nothing in it to lead me to this so-called cult. The file is open beside the journal. If the pattern continues, it means there'll be another death tonight.

The best way to track these people is to start at IES, but obviously they're good enough at what they do to avoid even the best security systems. So what chance do I have? In the file are included reports from IES investigators who tried tracking the group down.

Accounts of electronic devices suddenly going haywire, or shutting down entirely, as soon as the investigators felt like they were getting close. Accidents, like streetlamps falling over, or cars running on the sidewalk. Over the last three days I've followed up with every source I have, called every informant, and turned up nothing. I chuckle, feeling the numbing sensation of drunkenness creep over me. For a little while, I really thought I could do something. This time, I believed I could stop it from happening again. The girl's face swims in my mind, that eerily calm smile just before she touched the glowing surface of the Coil. I drain the bottle and hurl it against the far wall, where it strikes and clatters the floor unbroken. Nothing I can do. Nothing.

I hardly realize what I'm doing when I load a bullet in my revolver to replace the one spent on the guard at the Brant estate. I take a small copper ring out of my drawer, which has several wires folded around, it and a small silver battery. A silencer, pre-CoilTech, and very illegal. I slide it onto the barrel of the gun, and it contracts onto it with a snap, beeping to indicate it's active. Then, I'm strapping my shoulder holster on and donning my coat. It'll be sundown soon, and I want to be in position as early as possible.

The sky remains grey and clouded, threatening rain. I drive down twisting back lanes and through industrial neighborhoods until I find myself under the glow of the Coil, waiting in a shadowed alley facing the wall of IES headquarters. I sit, and wait. As it gets later, I drive around, making a circuit around the Coil without being in direct view of the facility. I catch glimpses of uniformed guards patrolling at street level and atop the building.

I park in a different alley, wait some more. Rinse and repeat, until it's all etched into my brain in full detail. This part of town, at this time of night on a Sunday, there were hardly any pedestrians, and none matching the descriptions of missing persons, whose faces I've done my best to study in the time I've had. I don't know what I hope to accomplish that the guards can't, and I call myself an idiot for being here, but I sit and wait at the ready nonetheless.

The few gulps I take from my flask are enough to make the time slip by easier without taking away my edge. Hours pass. I time the guard's intervals. He does a circuit every half hour. Parked not too far down from the guard entrance, I watch the regular sized steel door, equipped with a scanner for keycards.

When my watch strikes midnight, I still haven't seen anything. Rain taps a drumbeat on my windshield. The guard arrives at the security door and goes inside. I'm just about ready to start driving around again when something catches my eye. A flash of blue electrostatic light along the wall of IES. I open my door and lean out, looking up. Dark shapes rise up as though carried by lightning, darting over the top of the facility, leaping from the roofs of buildings across the street. Before I know what I'm doing, I'm running for the security door. I sway, realizing I may have drank too much after all. But I definitely just saw what I saw, insane as it may be.

Things started to happen around him. The maids words replay in my mind. I slip and crash shoulder first into the door, slamming my fist against the cold steel and hollering at the top of my lungs. When the guard cautiously opens the door he finds the barrel of my pistol in his face. I grab his taser and toss it out into the rain. "You have intruders," I say breathlessly. I grab his keycard. "Move." I shove him ahead of me through the grey corridors. "I need to get to the Coil."

"You're insane. If you do get out of here, it'll be in cuffs."

"The Coil!"

"You wanna die? Do you have any idea what kind of power output it has right now? This time of the week, no one goes near it."

"Why?"

"Because this is when the spare energy is harvested into the fuel cells we ship overseas. Touching it will kill you, hell, going too close to it might kill you."

"That's exactly why I'm here. Keep walking." I shove the barrel into the back of his head. Around a corner ahead of us, another guard emerges. He cries out and fumbles for his weapon. I blast him with a rubber bullet to the hand, knocking the taser away, then hit him with a foam cap, pinning him to the wall. The lights flicker. *No, not yet.* We move faster, rounding one corner after another, until we stand before a door very much like the one at the front entrance to the facility. "Stay here." I hit my captive with a gel charge to the feet, simultaneously sticking him to the floor and incapacitating him with an electric current.

The keypad beeps when I swipe the card, and the door swings inward just as I hear a shout from behind. I dash through, ducking just in time to avoid being hit by blue flashes from a taser gun. I spin around to see a guard rush through the door. Then a sheet of light appears out of nowhere, and he falls with a scream. I guess now I know what happens if you forget to swipe in on entry. I turn forward and freeze. I'm in the central courtyard, its center dominated by the Coil. The Coil's glow casts shadows off of the fuel cells lined up before it. Rain pelts the glass roof, and when I take a slow step my boots crunch on broken shards. Raindrops splash on my face when I look up to the stormy sky through the hole. It's only when I look down again that I see them.

They're standing in a row, making a crescent around the Coil, slivers of darkness on the backdrop of its pulsating light. And even though I can't see their eyes, I know all twelve of them are looking right at me. I'm back in time to ten years ago, frozen, petrified. A dozen pairs of eyes follow me each step as I make my stumbling approach. I feel the tingle of electricity, stronger now. Now I know it's not my imagination.

"The defective one."

"Will free us."

"We must find him."

They talk in turns, one after the other, in the same flat tone.

"The defective one will free us," they say, all at once.

Suddenly my throat is very dry, and I wish I hadn't left my flask in the car. "You don't have to do this," I shout. "Whatever you've been told, whatever you believe, it's not worth dying for."

"Only the defective one can free us," says one of the group.

"Do not interfere," says another.

"I'm here to help you. Let me help you find what you're looking for."

"Do not interfere," all of them in unison now.

I hit an invisible wall. With a shout I shove myself forward only to bounce back. When I rush at it again, the air crackles with blue static and I'm flung away to land on my back, body tingling. I get up, holding my pistol in a shaky hand. The group has turned towards the Coil. One of them is stepping closer to it as they chant.

"No!" I run as fast as I can, and I grab the one approaching the Coil and fling him away from it. It's only now that I realize how close I am to the thing. It's as if every last inch of my skin is crawling like its own living organism. .

"Do not interfere," they say.

I feel a slash of pain across my chest, and then another, as though I'm being hit with invisible whips. I fire my gun, but the rubber bullet deflects from its target with a flash of light. Then my gun flies out of my hand and hits the Coil with a crackle.

The fuel cells start to shift, dragging across the concrete, towards the Coil. I feel a tug in my pocket, and when I look I see my watch floating out, towards the wall of light behind me.

"We must find the defective one."

"Damn it, I don't know what you mean! Explain it to me!."

I grab the watch instinctively, and it pulls me with it, to the Coil. I fumble with the other hand to unlatch the chain. It snaps off my coat and tangles around the arm holding the watched, digging painfully into my skin. I'm pulled with it, hand first, to touch the wall of blinding light, and my world becomes pain, becomes burning agony as the power courses through me from my left arm. Then, all goes black.

———————

"Your drink, sir?"

I take the bourbon from the server with mumbled thanks. The good stuff, now. A hundred grand in credits in my account, I can afford it. I glance out at the ocean. I'm on a cruise liner, headed for… Well, headed for wherever I want to stop at, really. I sip the drink, and look again at the spiral mark on my left forearm. Like a burn that happened on the inside, which is essentially what it is. On the back of my neck is a similar mark.

After the pain of touching the Coil, I awoke to find cops and paramedics crawling all over IES headquarters, and Lin standing by my stretcher as I was lifted into the ambulance. Apparently, one of the guards I took out went ahead and called the police.

The things Lin told me were hard to swallow at first, but as she explained it, it started to make more and more sense. CoilTech, the bastards. Barely a decade into their operations with the Coil they started dabbling in behavior modification technology, testing integrated receivers in orphaned infants. After a testing phase, they started selling this new tech to wealthy parents, making the clients sign gag orders in case things went wrong. Which is, of course, what happened.

I guess they lost the paperwork on the early test subjects along the way, otherwise they never would have hired me to investigate the case. I now know the real reason I quit the force, or at least part of it. The software hooked to my brain was designed to steer me away from acting against IES. It only partially worked. In my case, there were clearly ghosts in the machine.

Those other poor souls, they were drawn to the damn thing and they had no idea why, all they knew was that if a faulty unit was brought closer to the source, it would short circuit the whole system.

They were fine, after I got zapped. But their memories of what happened after they snapped were gone. Luckily, the cops had more than enough evidence, with the Children of the Coil and the corpses in the freezer combined. Children of the Coil, that's what the news headlines are calling them.

Lin cooperated with the police, as much as she could without incriminating herself. One thing she managed was to get my pay wired to me before the company went down. IES is facing severe lawsuits from both the feds and the families of the Children, their former clients who claim they were extorted into selling out their newborn children. CoilTech is still in operation, taken over by the U.S government to complete the deal for the end of the year. All this crap, and the Coil is still going worldwide. I for one plan on being somewhere far away when that happens.

With a sigh, I reach for my drink. Blue static flashes briefly between my hand and the glass, and the bourbon jumps into my grasp, seemingly on its own. The lights overhead flicker. I chuckle mirthlessly, and finish my drink.

Super highways figure in again in our next story, prompted in part by the author's hour-long workday commute on Interstate I-70 in the American's heartland and partly by Norman Bel Geddes' super highways of tomorrow inside the GM Futurama exhibit at the 1939 World's Fair.

This is Mr. Hill's first published story.

There is No Way Like the American Way

By: Stephen Hill

Prepare ye the way of the Lord, make straight in the desert a highway for our God.

—Isaiah 40:3

Ash floated past young Hannah's eyes as the bonfire flickered against the starless sky. She followed the dancing movements against the night and pretended not to listen to Father arguing with the Stranger in the middle of camp, a look of quiet and dignified grace dressing her face and complimenting a defiant stance.

She could be my age, Hannah thought, taking in the Stranger's taller and more slender frame and she had a surety with the tall pole she carried with her that made Hannah jealous. Then there was the luxurious dreds of jet black hair spilling out behind her mask's hood. The mask sat on top of her head revealing a face free of pockmarks, with large brown eyes and clean bright teeth. The Stranger stood on one leg and balanced against the pole, regarding Father with an even indifferent gaze that Hannah did not like.

"I've never heard such babble," Father spat, raging around the bonfire as if he were going to raise the demons that Brother Jim was always preaching about.

"Those are the terms," said the Stranger.

"It's too much! We've barely enough for ourselves for the winter. And how are we to carry it all?"

The Stranger raised an eyebrow at Father, but then Grandfather interrupted, grabbing Father by the arm.

"Boy, now I was promised the Future, damn it all! Do not go ruining it for the rest of us."

"Thanks, Dad," Father said, yanking his arm free, "I'll remember that. I'm sure you won't mind carrying an extra pack for the long march ahead."

Grandfather grunted something unintelligible and walked off.

"Those are the terms," the Stranger repeated, with a touch more emphasis. "I do not personally care one way or the other. Perhaps you think you can find someone more qualified to lead you across the Way—"

"The Future!" Grandfather roared from the night. Hannah sensed it would be a night full of hooch and shuddered.

"—However, I sincerely doubt it. Perhaps you would rather stay here and wait out another winter, though I perish to think what you may look like after feasting on such paltry goods as what I am asking for in payment."

"We could go it alone," father mused.

"Ha! This you could do. I would give you three days at best, perhaps a week, and your progress would not be half the horizon. You do not know what terrors await on the Way. If you did, you would not be in the position you are in now. Let us be clear on where we stand."

Not everyone was clear on this point.

"There is no reason to leave the Dell," said Beadle Johnson, matron of the Second Family, so everyone could hear. "There's plenty to be had from the Burbs! We'll just have to push farther in is all."

"It's already taking scouts days to find anything worthwhile that's not also Dust-ridden," Father replied. "At this rate there will not be enough found to get us through the winter."

"And your solution is to cross the Way? Madness!"

A din erupted around the fire, and Hannah looked at her father and knew the Stranger had him. For all the torrents of anger raining around him and through him, the Stranger had him. Nobody made it across the Way without a guide. Everybody knew that. All the stories said so.

"Why has it always been thus?" Hannah asked, unsure of the spark that was lighting inside her.

The Stranger regarded her as if discovering an ant was crawling up her leg.

"Aren't we pretty today," she said.

Hannah felt the heat of anger upon her, felt her hand instinctively reach for the boomerang slung at her side. "You didn't answer my question, so I'll ask it another way. Why do guides not have a problem getting across the Way? There some sort of school for that? Sounds like you've got a nice setup."

The Stranger's pole that Hannah had been sure was stationary came from nowhere and Hannah felt a pain explode behind her knees. Hannah was looking up at the starless sky and seeing the cinders rise into the night, the wind knocked out of her. The Stranger's masked face began to eclipse the view, pole at the ready.

"That is how," the Stranger's muffled voice said, crystal covered eyes looking deep into Hannah's own.

"What. What is your name, Stranger?" Hannah breathed.

"Skylark," she said simply and then turned to look at Father. "Now I tire of this. If I am not needed here I shall move along."

"Wait, wait, wait," Father said, moving to help Hannah back up. "I agree to your terms." He turned to look over Hannah, gently brushing dead grass from her hair. "I have never seen anyone move that fast, let alone get the better of my Hannah like that. We need you and you know it. When do we start?"

"We start now."

Father looked into Hannah's eyes and she could see the worry in them. She felt ashamed, her eyes and cheeks burning. That such a girl could get the better of her!

"The Future!" cried a voice from the darkness.

The camps of the First, Second, and Third Families of the Dell were all abuzz with preparations. Two grand wagons built from Dust-free scraps were being made to carry provisions for the Families and their tithe to the Guides, all according to Skylark's strict and quite peculiar instructions. They were not to be wider than a man. In order to carry as much food as they were required, they would each be twelve Skylark pole-lengths long.

Hannah busied herself with the onerous task of moving cans from the First Family cache to the wagon build site. Her arms aching, sh noticed other, lesser, families of the Dell had come to view this spectacle of activity. Gnarled faces with mouths containing varying amounts of teeth chewed and gaped in the firelight. What was to become of the Dell once the First Family was gone? Who would fill the roles left by Father and Brother Jim?

Hannah had little pity for them. Any family outside of the first three were always an argumentative lot at best, would try and steal a rabbit you had just properly bonked on the head with your own boomerang for themselves, if given a chance. Greedy and beady eyes in the darkness looking at the light that would be leaving them soon. Hannah shivered and made her way back to Father and Skylark overseeing the wagon construction.

"First we meet Roadmaster," said Skylark.

"Roadmaster?" Father asked.

"Our leader. We will meet him where the Burbs spill into places of meeting before those spill into the Way. If you are worthy, we will continue."

"And if we aren't worthy?"

Skylark laughed, "Do not worry, I would not be here if it were not ordained. Still the meeting must be met."

Hannah did not like the idea of a meeting that had no merit. What was the point? She looked away from the great wagon that she and Father and her small brother, Rollins-Fred, would soon lash themselves to, along with the others of the Families marching across the Way, and did not trust her emotions, for they were everywhere, all at once.

The first thing you learn growing up, is you stay away from the Way. You stay away from the towns and the cities, too. The towns and cities will make you sick. The Way will merely kill you.

Grandfather spun tales of the Way and what it meant for those who knew how to read it. Magical passes one could perform that would bring all kinds of delicious food and wonderful clothes and move people to and fro and fulfilling every kind of need and bringing closer, ever closer the Future, bright and shining to everyone's beck and call. Grandfather regaled the children of the Dell with these tales that, for all their fantasy, were infuriating in their eagerness. In time, Hannah found herself wishing Grandfather to be quiet more often than he was.

Here were the facts as Hannah soon learned them: Life was a constant struggle due to the Dust, which seemed to be everywhere that old cities and towns were. Mother had got sick from the Dust and died not a year after Rollins-Fred was born. The Dust was outside of the Dell. But the Dust was also heavy and did not like to move, and if one was a good Silent Scout and did not stir it up, one could continue to live, and help the others to live as well.

Once upon a time, the first three families had fled the Dust and discovered the Dell. It was an expanse of wilderness mostly free of contamination. In the Dell there was grass that was not dead, and wildflowers, and blackberry bramble, and even rabbits. Spring water that was clean, along with bugs and nose flies and pit beetles. Old Scratch's reminders for sinners. The families thrived as they could, and in time others straggling in the world came to join them.

The Dell, however, was a trap. Albeit a kind one, for the Lord was, after all, merciful. It did not take long for family Scouts to discover its boundaries. It was surrounded by thick, though mostly dead, forest. And this forest was surrounded by roads. Roads that lead to towns and cities. Roads that lead to death.

That's what the children were told to keep them from exploring beyond their boundaries. Those were the facts that Hannah had grown up with. Tonight, as she hustled about moving boxes of canned goods from all the camps to the wagons, Hannah learned that it was the towns and cities that were sources of the heavy and vital foodstuffs, not some great hidden cache in the Dell ordained by the Almighty after all. It was the older kids, becoming Scouts with good filters on their head gear, hunting and gathering canned goods, and bringing them back, being careful of the Dust, being of light foot, that was keeping them alive.

Only the supply of these goods was running out. There were no cities. Only one town, and its storehouses where nearly empty. There were even other Dells, smaller than this one, and just as cramped with people. Winter was coming and the options were few. Father knew he could not impose order on hungry people. It was either move across the wilderness, and hope to find a new Dell, or take chances on crossing the Way.

Father, Brother Jim, and two of the Scouts from the Second Family went out in search of the rumored Guides after much heated discussion on the matter. As per usual, Grandfather's influence held sway. "We were promised the Future. Let's go find it." And so the Way it was.

The Way had no end as far as anyone could tell. Josephine Brubaker of the Third Family once told Hannah in confidence that she had seen the end of the Way in a dream sent to her by God. A vast white city where there was no Dust and no disease of any kind and towers full of people that shot right into the sky. It was full of machines that brought you all manner of things whenever you liked, and it was never dark and winter never came into that city.

Hannah had told Josephine Brubaker to stop drinking Grandpa's hooch and stealing his stories for her own. It had started a fight that Father had to resolve and Hannah felt bad about that, but she knew the truth. No one in any of the families had ever seen the end of the Way, let alone been across it.

Terrible noises came from the Way. All the scouts said so. Horrible rumbling and roaring noises like storms peeled at all hours of the day and at night there were strange yellow and white lights flickering against the clouds as well. Brother Jim said these were the battles of angels and demons and that only fools approach the Way without a pious heart.

Father had once told Hannah that if you stand next to the edge of the Way, it would go to the horizon in all three directions, and you wouldn't see anything but the Way. People became blind because of it. They got lost to the Way and they died.

This of course made Hannah and all the children want to see it all the more.

Being children, they were not as swift as the Scouts at the edges of the dead forest that surrounded the Dell, and they would be caught and rebuked in public, or invariably some kid from the Third family would tattle and then there would be switch whippings from Brother Jim in front of all the families and it was soon decided amongst the children that the Way was not worth it.

And now they were going to march right up to the Way, pretty as they pleased. Hannah felt the world was going mad. The truth she had grown up with was dissolving into something else, like mud sketches in rain.

She spotted a rabbit out the corner of her eye, and took her frustrations out on it with her boomerang. As she went to the carcass and began to dress it, she took a moment to look back upon the wagons, now both almost complete, and sighed. They were going to need this rabbit meat.

The Tithe was enough food to last half a year. They barely had it. But with Brother Jim and Grandfather whipping everyone into a frenzy of ecstatic expectation with talk of God and the Future, the excitement became a physical force of its own. They pulled stakes and headed into the deep night, the two great wagons moaning and creaking with each turn of wheel.

The children did not like being lashed to the wagons even though they were with their parents. It wasn't any fun, and it was the only way everyone could contribute to the momentum of the wheels for which there were no roads. The Scouts offered encouragement, cooing to everyone that it would get easier once through the woods. It didn't mean much to the kids, though, and with each passing moment Hannah found herself hating Skylark more and more. Skylark with her perfect skin and teeth and pole. Skylark who had broken the peace of the Dell with words and no proof.

"Look, Hannah," said a small voice to her side, "There's funny clouds in the sky!"

Rollins-Fred had managed to worm his body next to her and Hannah marveled at him. Somehow all that was going on wasn't having an effect on the skinny fair-haired boy; it was all adventure time to him. Trying to scare Rollins-Fred was a useless task, the boy didn't seem to understand the need for fear. Even Brother Jim had given up proselytizing in his presence. "My services would be better put trying to convert rabbits," Hannah had heard her uncle remark under the effects of Grandfather's hooch.

"Funny how, Rollins-Fred?" asked Hannah.

"They're huge!" said the boy, pointing.

Hannah followed his finger and saw on the horizon, storm clouds to the east, in front of the usual gray haze. That's exactly *what we need*, thought Hannah, then asked, "Just like Brother Jim's Behemoth, eh?"

Rollins-Fred made a noise and then replied, "Oh at least twelve bohweemuths. I hope it doesn't pop from being so heavy."

Their childish noise was receiving mean looks from the others. Hannah rolled her eyes and then leaned close to the boy.

"Me too, Rollins-Fred. Now, we need to travel in silence, OK? Could you be Silent Scout for me?"

"Of course," said the boy, twisting his lips with miming hands and making a face that made Hannah giggle.

They were approaching the periphery of the wood that had, for as long as Hannah remembered, served as a barrier from the Dust of cities. Even in the dawn light it was evident that the wood was dying, and not only because winter was on its way. It had a brittleness to it as if it were going to collapse into a pile of Dust itself.

Skylark said something to Father and he brought the wagon train to a halt.

"It will not take us long to push through the woods and into the Burbs," he said, standing on the first wagon. "This is when things will start getting dangerous. You who have been scouts know this well. You who have not, keep your masks secure and clear, and look to scouts for guidance. Do *not* remove your masks for any reason. Do not pick up anything you see, no matter how useful you think it might be. Is anyone unclear on this? If not, I'll be happy to have Brother Jim talk to you directly."

No one volunteered their ignorance. Father nodded and climbed down. The Three Families pushed into the woods.

The air was still and with each step the silence of the Dell that had been their home for so long, retreated. Hannah resisted the urge to look back. She feared it would only break her heart. Besides, there were more pressing concerns, such as watching after Rollins-Fred. She had to set a good example for him.

Dead, dead, and deader still, the leaves and shrubs turned to dust under the trod of feet and wagon wheel. They made good time. What green there was, had turned to brown, and the brown was turning to reds and grays. Barely an hour had passed.

The Burbs came on them like a dream. One moment it wasn't there. The next it was.

Square dead lawns surrounding square dead houses, all bound by square dead concrete paths both narrow and widespread out before them towards a thin line of charcoal that swallowed the rest of the horizon to the east and to the west.

There was litter on the paths.

"Vehicles. That's what they're called, Hannah, isn't it?"

"That's right, Rollins-Fred. Planes and trains and—"

"Automobiles!"

"If you don't mind," Skylark said, materializing out of nowhere and startling Rollins-Fred into Hannah's cloak, "We've got more than enough troubles in our future that will kill us swiftly, if they hear us. Do you understand?"

Hannah stared deep into Skylark's eyes for a moment and saw no fear in them. *She isn't afraid,* Hannah thought, *She is relieved. Why lie about the danger?* Hannah nodded curtly and Skylark withdrew to the front of the wagon train. "We must try and stay quiet," she whispered to the boy.

Rollins-Fred nodded into her cloak and then resumed walking. Hannah could see tears in his mask glinting in the morning light. She also discovered a deeper level of hatred than she had ever known.

Hannah found their lives sticking to the grid of concrete to be disappointing in its calm. The Dust was everywhere and if you were stupid it got in your lungs and you died, but if you were careful you could scavenge for canned food and feast. Next year she would have been old enough to join the Scouts and collect food for the Families, and if she was very lucky, perhaps find books and toys for the children. But then Father had said all of this was now empty of resource they could use. Was she herself empty of purpose?

Dead concrete flowed from house to house to dead streets filled with dead cars and trucks. The mighty chariots that were to bring about prosperity for all were now lifeless hulks, their tires flat, their windshields covered in Dust.

Hannah longed to see one move. Longed to open one up and see how it worked. Longed also to see inside a house or to find a supermarket like Father had before she was born. Hannah longed for something other than the stillness that permeated everything about the Burbs. Even the Dell had more going on than this place.

The flow of concrete in the Burbs was impossible to ignore. Like capillaries in the body, they were ever building into larger and larger boulevards when they first spied it, impossible to ignore once seen, it was the On Ramp of the Way. Someone was waiting for them at the bottom. A large group of someones.

Hannah was unsure of their number, but there was at least ten for every one of the Family members, all dressed in black skins and wild hair styles. Father always had everyone shave their scalps to stave off lice. This thundercloud of people seemed not to be concerned with such hygienic matters. They all carried poles like Skylark's and they were stomping the poles into the concrete with a driving rhythm.

At the center of the black cloud of people was one taller than the others. He was tall because he rode on the back of a beast, and his facemask was adorned with all manner of feathers.

"A horse!" Rollins-Fred whispered in awe. Exclamations and sighs spread through the wagon train as they saw the strangers, and the animal at their center standing proud with a mask on its head, stomping its hooves with nervous energy. It was as black as the skins worn by the others, but shiny and vibrant in the sun.

Skylark proudly led the wagon train to the black clad Guides. Hannah noticed that the way they had positioned themselves was a shape very much like her boomerang, with the big man on the horse front and center. He seemed to take notice of Skylark, and edged the horse from the wedge of leathered men and women towards her. With a jerk of the reigns he had the horse bow at Skylark and then the beast started sidestepping around the wagon train.

"Hail, Skylark! Is this the sorrowful group of which you sent me word?" The man's voice was like thunder, and the silence of the Burbs seemed only to amplify it.

"It is indeed, Roadmaster. I judge them worthy of our assistance across the Way." As she said this, Skylark moved to stand by Hannah and laid her hand on the girl's shoulder. Hannah jerked away and felt her other hand instinctively going for her boomerang.

"Do you indeed?" roared Roadmaster with laughter. "Perhaps you'll let me be the judge of who is worthy and who is not, little bird."

The rest of the Black Cloud Guides, their name that formed in Hannah's mind, laughed along with him, and as they laughed, Hannah noticed Roadmaster looking right at her with cold blue eyes that pierced her heart.

Father seemed to see it as well and stepped forward. "I was given to understand," he said, slowly and pleasantly, "That worthiness was not a requirement to cross the Way. Only that we were to bring the necessary payment."

The cold of the blue eyes evaporated and a pleasant mask fell on the pock marked face of Roadmaster. *This man is dangerous*, Hannah thought, and couldn't take her eyes off him. Rollins-Fred grabbed her cloak tighter and was whispering something about nightmares.

"You are the leader of this group?" asked Roadmaster.

"Yes," Father replied.

"What do you seek from the Way?"

"Merely passage," Father said after a moment.

More laughter erupted from the Guides.

"You are a leader of fools then, old father," Roadmaster replied, high upon his horse. "The world is full of death and you would seek an early audience in Death's domain?"

Father said nothing but kept a level gaze at Roadmaster. Seconds dripped by. Hannah braced herself for trouble.

It never came. Roadmaster regarded Father. "No one comes to the Way except through me. No one crosses the Way except by my grace. Have you brought the Tithe as specified?" he asked.

"Indeed," Father replied and waved his hand over the two great wagons.

Roadmaster gave the scantest of looks to the burden and then boomed so that everyone could hear, "Excellent! Over the next several days we shall guide you across the Way."

He began sidestepping the horse around the Families once more. The Black Cloud Guides began whooping and hollering and beating their poles in contrasting layers of rhythm that Hannah found terrifying and thrilling. The adults all seemed to relax a little. All except Father.

"We of the Guide Union shall proceed before you pilgrims," Roadmaster continued, "And Skylark shall heed our signals we send to the clouds, and you will be delivered into safety. We depart now ahead of you. Skylark shall bring you to the great On Ramp. We shall take the first half of the Tithe now as a measure of your faith in us. We shall take the second half once you've been brought safely across the Way and to the promise of a better tomorrow!"

Cheers erupted from the families, loud and long. Hannah's stomach felt ill. Father looked grim.

"The Future!" a voice called from the throng.

The On Ramp took three hours to climb. It was easily a hundred feet wide and Rollins-Fred was so tired Father carried him on his back most of the way. The throng of Guides easily moved the first cart up the ramp and out of sight with a speed and efficiency that left Hannah doubting her eyes. It also reinforced the notion that as far as the Way was concerned, the Guides were in charge.

Over the hours that passed, Hannah felt her ears pop, and her calves and thighs were sore from the effort. Even with all the Families focused on one wagon, towards the end of their climb it felt as though there were ten carts behind them. The view at the top, though, was worth it.

Behind them lay the Burbs, now tiny and somehow even pleasant to look at. They were like toys Scouts would sometimes bring back. Hannah fancied herself a giant. Ten steps would likely get her back to the Dell. How many steps for a giant over the Way? She turned to look upon it.

She could not stop looking. It went forever to the horizon in every direction from their feet. Though it was very flat, it was not perfectly so; in places there was a roll to it, like soft hills and meager valleys. Everywhere written upon its gray surface were dashed lines racing to the left and right horizons. A harsh breeze blew also from left to right, heated by what sun did pierce through the clouds. Specks of Dust flitted on that breeze. Hannah looked out on that bright gray horizon with its Dust devils whirling in the midday heat and grew afraid.

Skylark stood with two Guides who were waiting for them at the top of the On Ramp. She watched Hannah for some moments and then said, "The Dust is only the first danger. There shall be others. These families of yours must stay together as one as we cross the Way. You should try and stay in the middle of the families."

"Why are you telling me this?"

"I want you to live, that is all."

Liar, Hannah thought as Skylark withdrew and began speaking with Father.

Skylark stood upon the wagon and announced, "As we cross the Way, you will see signs. Do not speak of them. They are not for you to understand. They will be in the sky. They will be pillars of smoke during the day and pillars of fire at night. They will tell us how to move. You must move as one or you will be lost and our covenant shall be broken. I will not have any questions. There, look and see, our first column of smoke has arisen. We move now."

Everyone looked to her left and saw an incredibly tall column of green smoke climbing into thin air. It spiraled and banked and then disappeared into gray. Skylark and her two cohorts encouraged the blob of Families forward.

"Blessed be the Way," cried out Brother Jim.

The going was slow and tedious and as nightfall approached, Hannah was sure it was pointless. There was nothing on the Way but a bunch of Guides playing games with whatever was making the smoke. Brother Jim and his flock would praise every single one of those columns and Hannah was getting sick of it.

But still they would stop, they would go, they would turn left and then right and then right and the back forward and stop again. And now this close to sunset, the Way was all there was. Every direction was filled with it. There was only the Families and the Way and the darkening sky.

Hannah's patience was at an end. She was going to tell Skylark exactly what she thought about her whole charade and get some answers. She started to move away from the other children but then stopped. Everyone stopped. A column of violent purple smoke was racing towards the sky to their left.

"Damn," said Skylark, "Everyone! Single file right now!"

Hannah saw the lights before she heard the noise. A long line of bright white light was cresting a hill on the undulating Way. And with the lights came a rumbling sound, dull at first, growing in pitch and trembling the pockets of dust that swirled in the wind.

"Do not move from the line," Skylark commanded.

Hannah could feel a rumble under her feet, the breeze now a wind rushing in front of her and behind her and soon there was nothing but white light and roar-filled ears, and Rollins-Fred was screaming into her robes that he wanted picked up but it was not going to happen, Hannah knew it must not happen, and the lights were upon them in the front, and behind, and they were rushing past, and the pitch of the roar changed as they rushed, and a giant wind sucked and tugged at them, trying to pull them apart, and Hannah could see that they were all boxes of metal and glass—cars! Trucks! This is what they did! This was how they moved!

Hannah looked hard into the speeding roaring vehicles and saw nothing but bleached and hairy skulls grinning back at her, skeletal fingers stuck to the glass windows, pleading to get out and Hannah thought what possible hope could the Families have if souls moving this fast could be trapped so completely.

An age went by and finally the screaming stream of vehicles were gone in a dreamy haze of soft red lights, the white lights illuminating the cloud-heavy sky. The darkness that followed was a more complete darkness than Hannah ever experienced. She heard someone crying and realized it was herself. She was not alone. Rollins-Fred sobbed into her hand. Waves of anguish filled the Families and spilled from them. A fiery pillar of yellow and orange shot into the night sky to their right. Skylark and her nameless companions lit and attached torches to their poles. They meandered about the Families and hollered for everyone to press on.

Now Hannah understood why the wagons were built so stupidly awkward and narrow. Anything wider would have been ripped apart by the wave of cars and trucks. Hannah marveled at the prescience of the Guides, but was still terrified of what she saw inside the vehicles. Seeing Skylark stalk by her did not help her mood.

"All those people in the cars and the trucks, they're all dead," Hannah said.

"You're not," replied Skylark.

Hannah wanted to scream and shout at her. She didn't know what to scream and shout about. There was only anger, and the night didn't care and the Way cared less and all the people around her were just as tired and angry as she was. The Families continued on the Way in the torch-lit darkness. It was all they could do.

They continued following pillars of fire well into the night. Hannah could barely keep her eyes open. Father had taken Rollins-Fred and other adults took their tiny ones as well. He embraced her and said he was glad she was alive and was sorry that all of this was happening. He told her she was being very brave and was proud of her. Hannah could hear the anger in his voice and was happy it wasn't for her. Secretly she hoped to be awake when it finally spilled over on Skylark and Roadmaster and all the other stupid Guides.

Twice more in that night they had to straighten their ranks into a column as evil green flares shot into the night sky. Twice more Hannah looked on as faces of death rushed by her and threatened to suck her along into oblivion. And when she was sure she was going to stop where she was and move no more, a bright white light shot into the sky.

Skylark and her comrades gave out a whoop of joy. "Towards that light, all of you. This is what we have been marching for."

There was a sudden surge of energy in everyone. How was it even possible that their journey was so close to being over? Was this real? Was Hannah dreaming? As the white light faded their eyes spied a vast yellow and red warmth of many bonfires, warm and inviting. As they drew near, Hannah realized the place they approached was filled with more people all clad in black, more people than had greeted them at the On Ramp.

The Families were noticed by these people and they were hailed as old friends, long departed; what took you so long? Come! There is a feasting to be had, and cider to be drunk and fires to be warmed by! Rest and be refreshed brothers and sisters! You have traveled long but your worries were over!

"Over?" asked Father to one of the revelers.

"Yes, over," said Skylark, taking his arm. Hannah stood close by, she wanted to hear this answer as well.

"Where are we?" asked Father.

"It is a place of safety."

"How can anything be safe on the Way?"

Skylark smiled and shook her head. "Before us, there was a great crash. Many of the vehicles piled up together, becoming immobile. All the other vehicles moved on their own, in time, around this sacred space. The Guides found it. It is ours. And all the fruits of the Way are ours as well."

Hannah joined her father in having her mouth agape. They both looked at each other, and then around where they stood. "Camp" was not large enough a word. This was a town filled with stacked walls of tires and containers from the back of trucks. Spilling from the containers was more canned goods and boxes of all manner of things than Hannah could believe. Campfires undulated into the distance, and in their flicker Hannah could see other walls of containers and tires and barrels. The Dell had never had such wealth. This was civilization as it was before, only… transplanted.

"It is time they had the bigger picture, Skylark," boomed the voice of Roadmaster from across the merrymaking. He emerged from the fire-lit darkness, and though he was no longer riding his horse, it was evident he was still very tall. "You have reached the middle of the Eastward Flow, or as we prefer to call it, Damascus. There is nothing for you on the other side, only more death, like what you left behind."

"This is not what we agreed too!"

The Families were upset. How could they be tricked so, and then greeted as brothers and sisters?

"You had no idea what you asked for," said Roadmaster. Hannah could smell the cider on his breath from where she stood. The big man's demeanor had changed. The reservation Hannah had seen yesterday was gone. "You have no knowledge of the world beyond your precious Dell. You are like infants pleading for more suck at your mother's breast. The teat ran dry and now there is only the Way. Join us. Live, explore, contribute, and if you work very hard you will discover the Way is as full of Joy as it is of Terror, and we shall feast until the End of Days."

"This is madness," cried Father.

No one spoke for a moment. All eyes were upon Father. Brother Jim finally moved forward and stood next to him and pleaded, "It only makes sense, brother. Surely you can see it."

"How long," Father asked him, gazing into Brother Jim's eyes.

"How long, what?" asked Jim.

"How long had you been planning to give us to these Guides. It was like a miracle we found them, you said. Like a miracle that they knew exactly what we needed, and exactly how much to take from us. Now I asked you a question, *Brother.*"

"Long enough, Brother Mine. Long enough to see your wife die, God rest her soul. No more! I want to live! Brother, live with me in the Way."

"I…" but that was all that came out of Father's mouth. Hannah once again saw the look of being had come across his face. The look of not having a choice. Sorrow and anger welled up in her and she stood by him and said nothing. He was still holding Rollins-Fred.

"The future," said Grandpa from across the bonfire. He had found the mead and a girl. She seemed pleased to be holding him upright.

"That's right, the future," said Roadmaster, strutting over to where they stood. The cider smell was overwhelming and dawn's light was beginning to break behind the big man, and the shadows cast around his facemask heightened his menace.

The pit of Hannah's stomach dropped and a silence descended over everything. Roadmaster was looking right at her. Hannah did not like the look. Father woke Rollins-Fred and stood him on his feet.

"We must all talk about the Future today. About how your tiny Families shall join with the Guides. About how we will have a wedding feast like none that has yet been seen. We shall consecrate new ground on our honeymoon little one. You shall be the bride of the Future."

"I shall not," Hannah yelled.

"I am the first of the Guides," Roadmaster proclaimed, "As such it is my responsibility to choose a wife. To ensure the health of the Guides of the Way. I shall marry this little one and it shall cement our bond."

"That is not our way," Father said.

"You have no choice," Roadmaster replied, and lunged towards him.

Roadmaster's movement collapsed when Hannah's boomerang hit him squarely in the face. The big man cried out from the shock and whipped around to confront Hannah. His mask's faceplate was cracked and ruined.

Father jumped from his crouch and wrapped his arms around Roadmaster's head. He peeled back the big man's mask, and from his cloak, Father withdrew a small burlap sack and shoved it into Roadmaster's face and pulled the mask back down over his head. With a final kick to Roadmaster's groin, Father fell back onto the Way, and was beset upon by more and more of the Guides who began pummeling him with their staves.

Hannah discovered Skylark's staff was at her throat. Skylark's face was a tortured mask of fear and anger. Her eyes darted between Hannah and Roadmaster, confidence draining from them. *Were those tears?* Hannah thought, wondering why that, if they were, she didn't feel better about seeing them.

Roadmaster started to spasm and convulse and finally ripped his mask off. His face was covered in Dust. Bulging red eyes dumbly searched everywhere for relief from the pain. How much Dust he had inhaled was uncertain, but that sack was no longer full.

"Fool!" the big man rasped, a plume of Dust venting in the morning sun, causing people to dart away by reflex. "Do you think the Dust of the old world can defeat me? I am the Hand of the Way! I am the fruit of its impenetrable vine. What is greater than the Way?"

At that moment they heard it. They all heard it. Low and rumbling, a buzz like all the world's insects that persisted in spite of the Dust, a buzz that could fuel nightmares for the rest of time. It was in the sky, beyond the mountain of ruined cars and trucks and cargo containers, and they heard it and then they saw it. Low and slow it pierced the clouds and Hannah reached for her boomerang and longed to feel its shape in her hand, but the weapon had transcended the Way and she saw it, in the sky roaring as big as anything could be on this earth. Glass and metal glinting in the morning sun and whirligigs spinning with such fury they looked like wheels of crystal, and all along its center two massive pods strung under that stupendous boomerang simply hanging in the air, heading right for them, all low and slow.

"Look," said Rollins-Fred, "There's an airplane in the sky."

Up next is a story comprised of dualities. A story that begins and ends at the 1939 World's Fair. A story that is both intimate and grandiose in its scope. And a story that is, above all, a story of humanity.

Mr. Ham received First Place in the Science Fiction category for a previous version of this story in the 2013 Writer's Digest Popular Fiction Awards.

The Mobius Comet

By Craig J. Ham

The girl and her father stood at the base of the statue. "The Astronomer," was a large plaster man who towered above the crowds making their way through the World's Fair near the base of the spiraling path known as the Helicline. The giant figure was naked in the style of Greek statues, held a dodecahedron in one hand, and appeared to be searching the heavens above him.

"What's he looking at?" asked the girl.

"The stars."

The faint red orb of a distant plane winked slowly across the milky blackness and the girl felt suddenly lonely.

Her father reached down and gently took her hand, pulling her close to his side.

"Is he looking for your comet?"

Her father laughed, pushing his hat back on his head the way he always did when he was in a good mood. Moonlight sparkled in her father's teeth as he spoke.

"It's not my comet, Sweetheart. Someone else saw it first."

The girl looked back up into the night sky. "What does the comet look like?"

"Like a fuzzy star with a cotton tail."

She giggled as she imagined it.

"It's right over there". He knelt beside her and pointed as she followed his arm to a faint smudge of light near the crescent moon. She strained her neck, squinting.

"It'll look much larger in the telescope over at the pavilion."

"How come it looks fuzzy?"

"Because it's a big rock covered with ice, and as it flies though space, the sun melts the ice into steam. The steam makes it look fuzzy."

The girl imagined a huge snowball flying through space.

Her father knew a lot about stars. Sometimes he woke her up in the middle of the night and let her look through his telescope for hours. At least he used to. He didn't go out much anymore. He was tired and slept a lot of the time. Her aunt, who was at the house every day lately, said her father was sick.

He had brought her to Flushing Meadows Corona Park, in Queens, to the World's Fair. The year was 1939, and people from all over the world had come to see the wonders of science and the promise of the future.

On their way to the Time and Space pavilion her father stopped and studied another statue – one with three women standing beneath a tree that supported a large beam. One was holding a spindle of what looked like twine, a second was holding the twine out in both hands, and a third was cutting it.

"What's that?" the girl asked.

Her father didn't answer right away. He squeezed her hand for a second, knelt down next to her, and pulled the brim of his hat forward on his head.

"It's a sundial." He looked over at her puzzled expression. "You can tell the time by the position of the shadow it throws down. In the daytime of course."

The girl moved in for a closer look.

"I don't understand. Who are those ladies?"

"They are the Fates. The statue is called 'The Three Fates'."

The girl didn't understand, but nodded her head anyway. Her father continued.

"The twine or thread they hold represents time. Our time. The first woman here, Clotho is her name, is giving us the time. This represents our birth. Her sister, Lachesis, is holding the thread out, measuring it for us. She stands for things that happen to us, things we can't help or control… like disease."

The wind whistled around the girl's legs and she shivered as she looked at the third figure, cloaked and hooded.

"The one sitting on the ground scares me."

"She's supposed to," said her father. "Atropos. She's cutting the thread. Cutting our time. She represents death."

Her father looked at her for a few more seconds without saying anything. Then he put his hands on her shoulders and patted her.

"Come on, let's go look through the big telescope."

They continued down the concourse, through the throng of visitors, in the crisp air of the evening.

"Remember I told you about my friend Frank?" asked her father. "Do you remember what he said about the big comet that killed the dinosaurs?"

She nodded.

The girl stopped suddenly.

"Are we going to die like the dinosaurs?" she asked, starting to panic.

"No, honey, the comet that's passing by is not going to hit the earth. It's nothing for you to worry about."

She shook her head, satisfied.

"Well", he continued, "not all dinosaurs died when that comet hit the earth. Some of them are still with us."

"They are?" she stopped again, lowered her voice and peered up at him. He stopped as well, looking down at her.

"Yes, we call them birds."

"Birds? Birds aren't dinosaurs."

"Not any more," he said. "Over millions of years some of the dinosaurs that survived the comet slowly changed into birds. At least that's what Huxley argues – and I believe him."

"Who's Huxley?"

"A scientist, like Frank."

They continued on. The girl tilted her head at her father. "Birds are dinosaurs?"

"The dinosaurs had babies, and those babies had babies. Every once in a while the babies were a little different. Slowly, over time, the differences were more and more noticeable. Their tails disappeared, their teeth changed into beaks, and after a while they became birds."

She narrowed his eyes at him, thinking he might be teasing her, but his eyes weren't smiling.

"They look different," he continued, "but deep down, they're still dinosaurs."

She thought about this for a moment.

"I didn't know animals could change like that, into other animals."

"They can. That was what they are trying to show in so many of the exhibits here. Everything changes over time. That's the way things work. Animals are born, they have babies, they die…but nothing ever really disappears. It only changes form. Over time, the ice on the comet becomes steam, dinosaurs become birds." He paused to think for a moment. "The way they look changes, but everything that ever existed on earth is still with us. It's just in a different form."

The girl frowned. "I don't understand."

"Look at this." said her father. He stopped and kneeled down. He searched the ground, and picked up a small sand cricket from below one of the small trees.

The girl edged closer to where her father was kneeling and frowned at the remains of the singed creature in her father's hand.

"This cricket still looks like a cricket, like it did in life." He turned it over with his other hand.

"Yuck" said the girl.

"After it lays here awhile it will slowly fall apart and mix back into the earth. That's what happens to things like crickets when they die."

"That's sad", remarked the girl.

"Yes, it is, but the cricket mixes with the earth and becomes part of something else, perhaps the grass. What was once a cricket becomes something else."

"And," he said, "even more importantly, it probably left some baby crickets behind; so the cricket lives on through his babies, through his children."

"Poor baby crickets."

Her father looked sad and didn't say anything for a few moments. Then he continued. "In other words, honey, life never really ends, it just continues as something else – something new. Life is always changing and rolling forward like a great wheel that never stops. They call it the 'circle of life'."

He stood up again. "That's what that statue was about. Like our comet. It changes shape over time. It travels in a huge circle around our sun, once every quarter of a century or so." He nodded up at the sky. "When they first saw the comet, someone wanted to name it after a mathematician who thought about time and space and circles that never end."

"I know, I remember" interrupted the girl. "After I told my teacher we were going to look at the comet, she said it was going to be called the 'Mobius' comet. This Mobius guy was famous because he figured out how an ant could walk on both sides of a strip of paper whose ends were glued together, and get back to where he started without crossing an edge. She said there was a scientist who said this comet moves in a weird way like that around the sun. She drew a picture of it on the board."

Her eyes lit up. "Wait a minute."

She slid her satchel off her shoulder, rummaged around, and pulled out a long strip of paper, twisted once, and joined end to end.

"See", she said. Holding it with one hand, she traced her finger slowly over its surface with the other, hoping she was doing it just like the teacher.

Her father leaned down closer to watch as she continued. "No matter where you start…no matter which side…if you stay on the path…keep your finger on the paper, you can't lift it up. You move over both sides of the paper and end up back where you started."

She stopped and beamed a smile at him, her finger again at the "X".

"And so you do," he replied.

A little while later they were both looking into the eyepiece of the 36-inch telescope made by a Mr. Lutz, who was kind enough to let them look for the comet. He was surprised that the girl knew that it was located in the constellation of Cetus. Mr. Lutz asked her if she knew the name of the comet. He smiled when she called it 'the

Mobius Comet,' telling her he liked that name better than the other comet 35P Herschel-Rigollet.

She stood with her father, holding her hands behind her back, and looked into the eyepiece.

"It does look like it has a fuzzy tail," said the girl.

"I'm really glad we have this time together," said her father.

"Me too," said the girl.

A few weeks later, the girl's father died.

She missed him terribly. At first she kept thinking that it was all a bad dream and that she would wake up, but every morning the pain was there to greet her.

She didn't want to leave the cemetery after the funeral. It was raining. It felt wrong to just leave her daddy in the wet ground and walk away. At the house later that evening, she snuck into her father's closet and smelled his shirts.

The girl was sent to live with her aunt.

Many nights when she went to bed, she would look at the stars through her window and remember the trip to the World's Fair. It was their last real time together. She still talked to him.

Her mother had died when she was too young to remember, and she had been used to not having a mother. Now, she thought often about how unfair it was that other children still had fathers.

Her aunt gave her back the Mobius strip she had given her father that night. She said she had found it carefully folded in his wallet. She was also given her father's telescope. She treasured it, and used it to look at the stars and talk to her father as if he were beside her on evenings when the sky seemed too big.

Her heart ached for her father and she thought she could never be happy again. At times she was terrified because she couldn't remember his face. Other times it seemed as if she had just seen him yesterday. She would wake up from dreams of her father and cry until she went to sleep again.

The passing years dulled the pain of the loss. She kept his memory in a special place in her heart, a warm and quiet place from which she drew strength and a feeling of importance.

She found solace in books and study. Her favorite part of the day was dusk, when the sky was a pale blue and the first stars were appearing. She felt something solemn and rejuvenating about the onset of night. The triviality of everyday life was cleared away, replaced by the clear and complex beauty of the stars. It afforded her a solemnity of mind that gave her life perspective.

She became an astronomer, and kept a photograph of the statue of the astronomer that she and her father had admired that special night.

She married and had a son, named after her father.

When her son was still young, her husband, a colonel, was killed in Korea. She raised the boy on her own, and tried to show him the kind of love and attention that she had been given. From time to time she saw her father's expressions flicker across his face.

In 1964, she returned to Flushing Meadows, and walked the grounds where her and her father had spent those final precious hours together. The World's Fair of that year celebrated space travel, and she helped design the lunar base exhibit.

She found the spot where Mr. Lutz' telescope had stood, opened up the small suitcase she carried with her. She spent a few minutes aiming it at the right spot in the sky. It was difficult to see the comet through her tears.

Eventually, the day came when her son left home to live his own life. After that, her house was quiet and full of memories.

She continued to find sanctuary in books and study. She proved that the Mobius comet had entered the solar system with a speed that exceeded the Sun's escape velocity. The comet came from outside the solar system.

She called her son every Sunday and continued to worry about him as mothers do.

She became a grandmother.

Several years later, she returned alone to the park at Flushing Meadows. She carefully set up a small, dented telescope on its' tripod and swung it across the sky, across millions of light years, until she found the fuzzy smudge of light. The comet had once again returned.

Night clouds passed silently overhead. She smiled as a cricket scuttled across the grass near her feet. In her mind's eye her father stood next to her and laughed with her. She remembered the gleam in his eyes from the lamplights, the way the wind gently whipped his hair. So long ago. She felt old and young at the same time.

She worked at an observatory through long nights and lonely years. When she felt the cold in her soul, she wrapped herself in warm memories of her father, her husband, her son, her granddaughter; memories flooded in a remembered light that outshone the dim gray of the present.

The big questions, once so important in her life, remained for her unanswered. Life had delivered its finest gifts to her in the past, but with that she learned to be content.

Her son and granddaughter visited from time to time, and their presence comforted her.

She still visited her father's grave once a year, left flowers, and talked with him about her life.

Each year passed more quickly than the last, and when she entered the final season of her life, her ability to recall the past began to wane. Eventually she found that she would awake as from a dream, without any memory of where she had been or what she had done. Her memories were reduced to a rapid succession of faces and events, a kaleidoscope of disjointed and confusing images. She swam in psychic formaldehyde, surfacing at moments into a bright glare of awareness, and then sinking back into a state of oblivion. Her thoughts and remembrances disappeared like morning dew, fresh with the promise of a new day, disappears before the rising sun.

During one of her lucid moments, when she returned to herself, she was sitting on a park bench, with hair the color of winter frost, listening to the distant sound of children's play and the rustle of leaves among the weeds at her feet. It seemed to her at that moment that her life had passed away like a night vision, a blur of nebulous forms and images on the edge of wakefulness.

One day she sat in a wheelchair at the window of her room in the nursing home, gazing out at the grounds, the land and sky blending together into shadows of gray. On her bed sat a worn-out satchel. She sat patiently, looking at her own reflection in the window; a ghost image, insubstantial, tufts of her blue-gray hair jutting out at odd angles in a wispy halo. She was wrapped in a cocoon of blankets, waiting for someone to come, like a baby bird waits for its' mother. Presently a large man came and took her away, out of the room, through the halls, and out the front doors to a car parked at the curb. A woman who looked vaguely familiar was standing by the car. She said it was cold for a summers' evening. Then the woman smiled at her, kneeled down and carefully wrapped a scarf around her head, smoothing down her hair as she did so.

Then she was at a park. The same young woman arranged a small telescope on a metal folding table. All of it seemed so familiar—the glittering sky, a cool wind against her face. She was wheeled forward. The young woman pointed to the eye of the telescope, supporting her as she instinctively strained forward and passed a few moments looking through the eyepiece.

A glimmer of recognition flickered on her face as she settled back into her chair. Like a wave slowly lapping against the shore, depositing a piece of driftwood, the image of her father emerged from a jumble of images floating on the periphery of her consciousness. A brief surge of memories flooded back with it, startling her like a bright light turned on after a nightmare. Her father stood silhouetted against a starry sky; his eyes gleaming, the wind gently whipping his hair as he ran his hand through it, putting his hat back on and pushing it back. She saw the crease in his pants, and felt old and young at the same time.

Moonlight reflected on the surface of an old statue nearby, something familiar, and for a moment, she was a little girl again. The images however, receded away quickly, like waves of a tide, and she settled back in her wheelchair.

Later that night, she awoke suddenly in her bed. Her mind was clearing again. She felt a slight dizziness, as if she was looking down from a great height, poised on the edge of a chasm. Then, something wonderful. Her entire life washed over her in a single moment: lying sleepily in her mother's arms, her father's smile above her against a starry sky, the searing caress of her husband in the dark, the newborn glow of her son as he nursed, her granddaughter's parting wave as she drove off to her first day at school.

The wave passed. She let go. As her mind relaxed, she fell toward the brilliant light at the end of the tunnel.

She was buried next to her father.

Years passed.

The remains of the father had long since returned to the earth. Eventually, those of the daughter dissipated into the soil as well. Elements from both of them joined together and nourished a milkweed that grew between the stones. One cold night in December, the milkweed died, and the elements were released again into the soil.

Her son and granddaughter brought flowers to the graves on her birthday for years afterward, until they too passed on.

After a few generations, the lives of the father and daughter were forgotten by all who lived. All of their hopes and joys, deeds and loves, were compressed into a few names and dates in the public records.

The tombstones of the father and daughter were washed by the rains of a century, until the names disappeared. The cemetery itself was destroyed in a great earthquake shortly after the end of that century.

Elemental remains of the father and daughter washed into a river. Swirling to the bottom, some of the remains were buried in sand.

Centuries stretched into eons. Great upheavals rocked the earth. Plagues decimated the population. Some life forms disappeared from the earth. Mankind survived, and from time to time, flourished. History rolled on in great cycles, a single symphony resounding over and over with the same notes, like waves lapping over each other on the shore. Nations rose and fell, grew and fractured, like the light of the moon on a turbulent sea. The love of humanity waxed and waned, but still humanity endured.

Robotic probes were sent as emissaries to distant regions. Space travel became a commonplace.

The human brain, its geometry of thought and consciousness, were transferred with increasing success into more permanent systems, first silicon computers, then, organic creations of increasing sophistication. With virtual immortality, man left the earth and traveled out into the stars, taking other forms of life from their world to seed new planets.

The earth itself remained a shrine, a place of pilgrimage for its former inhabitants.

Over billions of years the earth's sun began to shudder and pulse. Then it began to swell, engulfing the innermost planet Mercury in boiling red heat.

On the earth, the polar icecaps melted and flooded the coastal lands. After more time, the oceans became steaming cauldrons of mist and fog that enveloped the earth with a noxious shroud, streaming across the surface in great billowing waves, flashing great veins of lightning.

The sun swallowed Venus, continuing its relentless, searing expansion.

Clouds raged impotently across the face of the earth, dissipating in withering heat. The red globe of the sun filled the sky. All that remained on the surface was parched and skeletal. No animals. No plants. No life.

A short distance from the planet, a fleet of machines floated, each inhabited by plasma intelligence, recording and transmitting images of the death pangs of their mother world. The planet was the womb and cradle of their race, nourishing them in the infancy of their species, before they transcended their impermanence, seeded other worlds, and harnessed the ability to warp the fabric of space and time.

In one final paroxysm the sun explbded, hurling a red shroud out into space. The heat blast razed the surface of the earth, searing and scorching what remained, buckling metal and melting rock. Red-fringed magma exploded from its' core and flowed across the land.

The beings that had once been humanity maintained their vigil, floating in ceremonious silence. The earth finally disintegrated, and the remains of its charred corpse were carried out into the cosmic ocean on the crest of a mighty solar wave.

The fleet, carrying the heritage of the world that had been, continued on its journey.

Great chunks of the earth floated and collided: pieces of the Appalachians, molecules of hydrogen and oxygen that had been the Ganges, organic molecules, the dust of kings and commoners, all returned to the fertile void from which they had originated. The ruins of Rome, the sands of Egypt, the verdant forests of Europe, the moon that had once hung over lovers, all that was art and beauty, vibrant and alive, careened outward, collapsing into chaos and washing out into the stellar sea, like grains of sand from a thousand rivers.

The sun, its life spent, receded into a shrunken vestige of its former self, a glowing ember flickering in the darkness.

The elements that had once been father and daughter were embedded in a small mountain of rock along with pieces that had been part of a Greek amphitheater, a Mayan temple, crystallized rock from Antarctica, silicon from the Saharan desert, remains of the Sphinx, and the bones of a whale. That which had been all these things floated in the silence of eternal night.

More time passed. In the distance appeared a glowing hole, outlined in swirling red, a discontinuity of blackness against the background of stars. Over time, the rock was pulled slowly, inexorably, towards this dark whirlpool, into the orbit of a binary star system.

One large star spun in a cosmic dance with a massive, dark companion, pulsing as its gas and matter were stripped off by the black hole.

As the rock approached, ice vapor streamed off in a long flowing veil as it too joined in the deadly, spiraling dance.

After a short courtship, the rock pirouetted into the hole that had been a star, and in a single moment, space and time merged, length became time and time became distance. The swirling matter became a tunnel through which the rock careened, warped, lengthened, broke and fused again. It emerged from the wormhole in a blinding explosion of light and energy, in another part of the universe, in another time, far distant from where and when it had entered.

The rock containing the ancient matter that had been father and daughter was eventually drawn into another cosmic dance, the orbit of a distant single star, and a spherical halo of rock and ice formed around it. Time and again it smashed and splintered against other chunks of debris and rock. It circled around this new star for millions of years.

The time came, on one of its orbits, that the light from the comet intersected a small crystal blue planet, pierced the dark side of the planet's atmosphere, and entered the shaft of a 36-inch reflecting telescope. Father and daughter peered into the telescope. "I'm really glad we have this time together," the father said.

"Me too," said the girl.

Later that evening, they stood by their car.

"I don't understand forever," the girl was saying.

"No one does, honey".

"No matter how long of a time I imagine, I never, ever get there". The girl held the Mobius strip up to her face and followed it around and around, over and under, with her eyes.

She settled her head against her father's arm and they both looked back out into the inky sky above them. The open void frightened the girl. It made her feel small. She moved closer to the warmth of her father's body and felt better.

"Thanks for bringing me to the Fair."

Her father smiled, and settled back against the car.

"I wish I could visit the stars," said the girl wistfully. "I wish you could take me there, daddy."

Feeling a little tired, she looked up at her father and pushed the Mobius strip into a heart shape. She held it up and giggled.

"Maybe I will someday," answered the father.

And he hugged his little girl under the expanse of eternity.

Electro makes his final appearance in our next story. From its beginning, modern household automation has been touted as liberating for the housewife, that mainstay of American life and advertising. Should anyone wonder then, that the programmers of household robots should take special care to ensure their primary demographic is satisfied?

Ms Cage writes science fiction and romance, with two published novellas, and one novel. Some of her stories have appeared in Alienskin Magazine. She resides in Britain.

The Robot Who Smoked

By Stephanie Cage

"We're getting what?" Ellen stared as her husband kicked off his shoes, shoved his feet into plaid slippers and parked himself in an armchair.

"A robot. Elektro Mark II. Does everything, even smokes."

Barrett flicked a switch on the chair arm and turned his attention to a wall-mounted vidscreen as if the conversation were at an end, which as far as he was concerned, it probably was.

"Smokes," Ellen echoed.

"That's what I said," Barrett agreed, toeing his slippers more firmly into place.

How ridiculous, thought Ellen. What was the point in causing a robot to copy humanity's most extreme demonstration of unnecessary consumption?

"Wait a minute," Ellen said, dropping into the armchair opposite and flicking another switch.

The screen went off and Barrett turned his attention back to her. She'd half expected him simply to turn the screen on again. They could have gone on like that all night.

"What? I thought you'd be happy. Taylor and Vivien have an Elektro. Riley and his wife have a Mark II."

"We're not Taylor and Vivien. Or your boss and his stupid wife. What do we need with an Elektro?"

"It can, I don't know. Help you with the housework. The cooking. Whatever the hell you do around here all day."

"Oh really?" Ellen gave him the look, the one she'd inherited from her mother that had always quelled her and Luke as kids.

It had worked on Barrett, too, for the first few years of their marriage. If they'd had kids, it probably would have worked on the kids too. But it didn't work on Barrett. Not anymore. Nine times out of ten he didn't even notice the look because his attention was on the vidscreen or the paper. The tenth time, he rolled his eyes in a way that was meant to convey that he wasn't a kid to be quelled with a look. Of course, the eye-rolling merely made him look even more like a sulky kid, but Ellen had never felt the need to tell him that. Come to think of it, there were a lot of things she didn't feel the need to tell him nowadays. Which might be one of the reasons why he had no idea what she actually did all day.

"Are you sure you wouldn't rather take it to the office? It could help with… whatever the hell you do there all day." Ellen laced her tone with bitterness, but if Barrett noticed, he just ignored it, as he ignored so many other things.

"Wouldn't be much help with claims management. They do have a brain, an electro-mechanical brain, but even the Mark II doesn't have a million micro-relays. That's not enough for the sort of complex analysis we handle every day."

Once again, Barrett sat back in his chair and flicked the switch. The wall screen lit up and filled the room with an advertisement for the latest self-drive car. This one had a built-in vidscreen above the dash so you could commute and conference at the same time.

"Pretty darned smart, huh?" Barrett smiled.

Ellen rolled her eyes and went out to check on dinner.

When she came back in with his tray, the adverts had given way to a news programme, which he proceeded to talk all the way through, mostly about how much better he and Riley would handle whatever minor crisis faced the government, police force or medical profession.

Sometimes she wasn't sure he noticed if she was there or not, as long as dinner appeared on time.

Maybe she could get the Elektro set up to handle all the household chores, and then she could just move out and wait to see how long it took him to notice.

She smirked.

"Did I miss something?" he asked, looking sideways at her.

"Why?"

"Nothing funny about the rising price of tungsten. It could force the price of most technologies up significantly. One of the reasons I thought we should get in on the robot market while we can."

"You're probably right, dear. Now that I've given it some thought, I can see that it could be quite useful."

"Good, good," Barrett said, in the tone of a man who'd just been waiting for the little wife to see sense. She was finding it hard to recollect what she'd ever seen in him.

Ambition, she thought, pushing her memory back to the day they'd strolled through the park under the freeway and watched the cars going past. Ambition and intelligence. He'd talked about how one day he and his colleagues would manage all the risks of driving out of existence. So much of what he'd predicted had even come true, and yet underneath it all, nothing seemed to change.

The wall screen and the food centre and the robovac were all supposed to have freed her to find self-fulfilment, but all they'd really given her was monumental boredom, and more things to keep an eye on and call the repair man out to. So why would an Elektro be any different?

Still, she did get a slight thrill out of telling Vivien that not only were they finally joining the robot age, but they were going straight to the Mark II. Apparently Taylor had told Viv that the Mark II had a much more sophisticated language engine, and you no longer had to be careful to phrase instructions around its limited vocabulary.

"You can even have a conversation with it," Viv gushed, and Ellen rolled her eyes inside where her friend couldn't see, thinking that in that case the robot had a head start on either of their husbands. Viv didn't seem to mind Taylor's obsession with work, but then Viv had little Johnny to occupy her attention.

Ellen had never told her friend how much she envied Viv's family life. Viv would be sure to egg her and Barrett on to start a family, but Barrett wasn't keen – 'expensive little beggars, kids, and so many things that you have to worry about' – and besides, how did you start a family with someone you never saw except when they were eating or snoring?

"So when's the miracle mechanical man arriving?" Viv asked.

"Next Tuesday."

"And when do I get to come and see it?"

"Thursday? When Johnny's at Future Leaders?" The name of his pre-school was another thing that made Ellen want to roll her eyes. Honestly, Barrett must be having a bad effect on her, because eye-rolling seemed to be her response to pretty much everything nowadays.

"Thursday it is. Think you'll have him house trained by then?"

"Who knows? Barrett says it arrives fully functional, but then they said that about the robovac too and it took six weeks before the vac knew the house well enough to stop bashing the legs of the dining table every time it went past."

Ellen had been tempted to remove the dining table just to stop the banging, but even though they always ate in front of the TV, she hadn't been able to bring herself to dispense with that symbol of family life. And, finally, the vac had learned to manoeuvre around it.

She wondered how the Elektro would be at getting around the house. Viv's seemed to cope well enough, though at nearly seven feet tall, it did tend to make a room feel crowded.

"You don't think it'll be too big?" she asked Barrett anxiously over dinner that night.

"What?"

"The robot."

"Apparently the Mark II is nearer six feet than seven. More human looking."

"Good," she said faintly, and went back to watching the documentary about the latest rocket ship which had opened up high-altitude runs between the US and Asia.

"I'm glad you don't have to go to Asia," she remarked.

"I think it would be exciting," he disagreed. "And I might get a chance when the merger goes through."

"Merger?"

"Yes, we're joining with Shanghai Claim Handlers, didn't I tell you?"

"No, you didn't. How long have you known this?"

"Oh, they've been talking about it for months, but it's only been official for two weeks or so. I didn't want to say anything until I was sure, but it could really open up some opportunities for someone at the cutting edge of the insurance industry."

Ellen wasn't sure insurance even had a cutting edge, but now at least the robot made sense. Barrett wanted to prove he was up with the latest technology. She just hoped they could afford it. Well, if all these new opportunities opened up, then that shouldn't be an issue. But how many of the new opportunities were real, and how many were just in Barrett's head?

"That's good, then," she said helplessly. Honestly, no wonder he never told her anything. After all these evenings frying their brains in front of the vid screen, she seemed to have forgotten how to have a sensible conversation. Maybe she could practice on the robot.

"Riley says I can come in late on Tuesday, make sure the delivery and installation go smoothly."

"That's nice of him," Ellen said, though privately she wondered whether it wouldn't be easier to get used to the thing if she had some time alone with it.

In the end, though, the delivery came so late that Barrett only had time to plug it into the wall point and start it charging before he headed off for a vid conference with his opposite number in Shanghai. Ellen could never understand why they had to trot into the office for these conferences when everyone had a vidscreen at home, but she'd long since given up arguing over the illogic of company rules. Barrett would no more admit that the company might make a mistake than he would admit he'd bought the robot more for his image than her convenience.

Ellen made her lunch while the robot was charging, and then sat down to read. She kept looking up, though, wondering how long it would be before the robot was charged enough to activate.

Finally she put down her book and eyed the humanoid form standing with its arm raised to jack into the wall socket. It was, as promised, less intimidating than the original clunky Elektro.

"Are you going to name it?" Viv had asked the previous day.

"I don't know. That might make it seem a bit too human," she'd said, but now she realised that she couldn't go on referring to 'it' as 'it.' There was definitely something masculine about the chunky body, chiselled face and arms and legs bulging with solenoids and relays.

"Mark," she said aloud now. It wasn't just an Elektro, it was an Elektro Mark II, and apparently that made all the difference.

"Did you address me?" a voice enquired. Ellen jumped, then gave a nervous giggle as she realised that she'd been startled by the very thing she was watching.

"I was talking to myself," she admitted, embarrassed, "but I think Mark would be a good name for you. Don't you?"

"Mark." He said the word slowly, as if testing the sound. "Mark." The second time, he tipped his head to one side, like a wine taster considering the flavour of a fine vintage.

Ellen raised her eyebrows. The programmers, it seemed, had done a fine job, not just of his language engine, but of providing him with convincing mannerisms.

"Is that OK?" she asked, wondering if she was crazy for considering a robot's opinion.

"Yes, I like it," he said, and although she knew he'd probably been programmed to be agreeable, she still felt a small thrill at his expression of approval. It was rare enough that Barrett approved of, or even noticed, anything she said or did.

"That's good. I am completely charged and ready to be of assistance. What would you like me to do?"

Ellen thought of Barrett's 'whatever the hell you do around here.' Could she get the robot to help with the cooking, the cleaning, the household finances? Would she still need to get a repair man out every time the robovac sputtered to a halt or the tap refused to stop dripping, or did the robot, Mark, know how to do basic repairs?

"I don't know," she confessed. "I don't know what you can do."

Was that really the problem, or had she just become so unused to being asked for her own opinions, she'd forgotten how to have one?

"I can perform basic domestic tasks and repairs, and simple administrative functions. I can converse, smoke and drink. There are additional modules for more advanced business purposes."

Ellen wondered whether that included insurance and claims, and whether Barrett had known about the business modules when he implied that she was replaceable by a robot and he was not.

"Could you get me cup of tea?" she asked, thinking she might as well test Mark out on something simple, get him used to finding his way around.

"Of course. Which way is the kitchen?"

She gestured towards the door.

Mark retracted his arm from the wall socket and followed the direction she had shown him. Even though she was used to Viv's Elektro, she was still slightly disconcerted by the robot's mechanical eyes. It was odd to feel watched by an electro-magnetic device. Especially one that talked like a person. She wondered if it was considered polite to keep your robot company while it did chores, or whether the whole point was to get on with other things.

"Should I talk to you while you make tea?"

"If you like," he answered, opening the kitchen cupboards one after the other and doing a quick scan of the contents.

She resisted the temptation to point out where the mugs were stored. He might as well learn his way around now as later.

"Perhaps you could tell me about yourself and Mr Bailey."

She jumped. How had he known about Barrett? Then she answered her own question. Of course, his name was on the ownership documentation, which was pre-loaded onto the machines.

"My name is Ellen," she began. "My husband's first name is Barrett. I don't think you need to call us Mr and Mrs Bailey." Whenever she heard those names, she thought of Barrett's parents. They were nice people, but old-fashioned even for their age. Barrett's father still drove a fully manual vehicle, and was one of the most vocal protestors against the plan to insist on basic automation for safety purposes.

"Nice to meet you, Ellen," Mark said, as he located the jug kettle and placed it under the tap. Although his fingers looked awkward, he seemed to have no difficulty managing the intricacies of the taps.

"Nice to meet you too," she responded, and to her surprise, she found she was telling the truth. Even though Mark's face had no expressions, she found that the modulations of his voice and the subtle movements of his head and shoulders enabled him to project an aura of friendliness that she found quite appealing.

"How did you and Mr Bailey, Barrett, meet?" he asked.

Ellen wondered who had thought to program him with conversational opening gambits, and how many he possessed. Would he have asked anyone the same question, or had he been taught that women preferred personal chat, while their husbands would rather discourse on the state of the economy?

"I'd just finished college," she began, "and I was working at a hotel reception desk and there was a big conference on. Barrett's firm was organising the event, and he was quite new, so his boss kept sending him out on errands. By the time we'd finished finding obscure gluten-free foods for health-freak guests, and a repairman for the car whose guidance system had gone wrong, and whatever else his boss couldn't be bothered with, he'd managed to charm me into eating dinner with him every night of the conference. He was very charming back then."

Ellen took the tea Mark handed her, and moved back to the living room. Mark followed.

"May I sit down?" he asked, standing in front of Barrett's chair.

"That's Barrett's chair," she said, "and this one's mine, so I guess the sofa is yours."

She sat down in her chair, and Mark sat down on the half of the sofa closer to her. He sat forward in the seat, hands resting on his knees, as if waiting for her to go on.

"How long have you been married?"

Even as she carried on talking, Ellen wondered why she was spilling out her life story to a metal case filled with relays and solenoids. Wasn't talking to a robot just one step up from talking to yourself? Still, she found she was enjoying the chance to reminisce without Barrett arguing with her about the way she remembered things. Their wedding day had been wonderful, and when they came back from their two week honeymoon having still never spoken a cross word to each other, she'd thought it an omen that life would be perfect forever.

"The irony is, we still don't speak a cross word to each other. Mostly, we just don't speak to each other at all, and when we do, we still don't say anything."

"How do you feel about that?"

Ellen wanted to laugh. Apparently somebody had known that a woman provided with a listening ear would always find something to say, and had given Mark the appropriate set of responses.

She knew he was just a machine, and that her answer would mean nothing to him, truly she did, and yet she couldn't resist answering.

"I feel lonely."

She hadn't known until she heard the words, how true they were. But, yes, she was lonely. Viv had Johnny, and Mr. and Mrs. Bailey the Elder might be boring, but they still seemed to enjoy each other's company, and she only had Barrett, the blank-faced.

"So lonely," she repeated, her voice sounding small and wistful.

"That must be hard for you," he said, and Ellen found she was noticing the slight mechanical hesitations in his voice less, and finding instead, a sympathetic richness in his tone.

"It makes me feel that something is wrong with me," she admitted, then looked down at her lap, where she found she had been twining her fingers into the fabric of her skirt. She untwisted the knots of crimplene and smoothed out the fabric, then let it go, and watched the wrinkles bounce back into place.

There was a pause, and she wondered if she had exhausted Mark's conversational abilities.

He lifted his head with a slight creak, thoughtfully, in the way that a human might draw a slow breath, and opened his mouth to speak.

Ellen's heart beat a little faster as she wondered how he would respond to her revelation.

"May I have a cigarette?" he asked.

Ellen let out another nervous titter at the robot's unexpected request. Apparently, the robot was causing her to regress to a school-girlish demeanour.

Whatever she'd expected from the robot at this point, it wasn't a request for a cigarette.

"I suppose so," she agreed, going to the drawer where Barrett always kept a spare packet of smokes. She pulled one from the packet, picked up a lighter, and took them over to the sofa.

"Should I smoke outside?" he politely asked.

"I don't suppose it matters. Barrett often smokes inside." She put the cigarette into his large metal hand, noticing the coldness of his fingers as they brushed hers. He was surprisingly dextrous, despite his size, as his fingers settled the cigarette carefully into place and held it out for her to light.

After a moment's hesitation, she sat down next to Mark and brought the lighter to the cigarette.

The tip kindled into a glow, and Mark settled back into the chair.

Ellen set the lighter down on the coffee table and settled down beside him.

"I am sorry you feel lonely," he said, as if the interruption of the cigarette had never happened. Ellen remembered wondering why anyone would want to make a machine that smoked. Now, she liked the way he focused on drawing smoke in and letting small curls of it out. The hypnotic rhythm seemed to absolve her from the pressure of responding, so that she could simply sit and enjoy the feeling that someone, something, she reminded herself crossly, cared how she felt.

"If I were a man married to a beautiful woman like you, I would not let you feel so alone."

"They've given you all the lines, haven't they?"

He breathed in smoke and blew out a curl. Barrett used to try to make smoke rings, she recalled. The room was beginning to smell of Barrett, the fresh smoke smell that surrounded him, rather than the stale smell that lingered when he wasn't there. Ellen had never taken up smoking. She suspected Barrett thought it was unbecoming in a woman, and wondered whether that was reason enough to start.

"I'm not beautiful," Ellen said. She didn't think it was false modesty on her part. She was ordinary at best, a bit on the plump side, not as well groomed as Viv, despite not having a child to distract her from the work of turning herself into the perfect hostess Barrett must have expected.

"Everyone is beautiful in their own way," Mark said.

She supposed it was a compelling message, and wondered whether the robots' point of view was the Corporation's way of subtly instilling a positive attitude in the public at large, or whether a rogue idealist among the programming team had sneaked their viewpoint in without the Corporation's consent. Either way, it was a nice thing to hear.

"You are very beautiful," he added, stressing the word 'very.'

In spite of herself, Ellen smiled. She watched him transfer his cigarette into his right hand, lean forward and shift the ashtray across the coffee table so that he could perch his cigarette there.

Then he leaned back, angling his body subtly towards her.

"I'm not," she insisted, as the years of Barrett's subtle denigration bubbled to the surface. "I'm ordinary. Dull. I'm not elegant like

Barrett's mum or glamorous like Viv or even clever like Barrett. I'm just me, and I might as well be nobody. Oh, why did he expect me to be anything special? I'm only human!"

"And human is a wonderful thing to be," Mark reassured her, but the tears were already welling up and nothing he could have said at that point could have stopped them spilling out, forming duller yellow circles on the soft buttercup fabric of her skirt.

After a moment she gave up fighting the tears and pulled out a handkerchief to sob into.

"Shh," he murmured, sounding soft and comforting and all the things that Barrett hadn't bothered to be since the early days of their courtship.

Instinctively, without thought, she turned into the strength of his body and let her head rest against the cool metal of his shoulder. She'd half expected him to smell of machine oil, but he hardly smelt of anything at all, just a faint, comforting cleanness which might have come from either his freshly washed clothing or his body itself.

"Shh," he said again, and this time one metallic hand came up and began to stroke her shoulder with slow, steady movements.

After a time, she swallowed back her choking sobs, and once they had subsided she asked, "I won't make you rust, will I?"

"No," he said, and she wondered if she heard a hint of amusement in his voice. "The metal is lacquered so that I won't be affected by washing up water, or rain." Then he added, after a moment, as if it was surprising to him, "or tears."

"I'm sorry," she said anyway. "I didn't mean to cry."

But she didn't move away, and he just there, infinitely patient in his metallic strength, watching the cigarette burn down.

After the last curl of smoke had faded away, Ellen heard the sound of a car pulling into the driveway.

She stood up and brushed down her skirt, nervously, as Mark also got to his feet.

"I don't look as if I've been crying, do I?" she asked.

"Not at all. Here." He took her handkerchief and wiped the corner of her eye, then stepped back to examine his handiwork.

"Perfect," he pronounced, and for a moment she thought the tears were going to well up again.

She swallowed hard and went to the kitchen door.

Barrett got out of the car, fairly bouncing with enthusiasm, and for a moment she thought he was excited to see her at the door.

"It's official," he sang out, "You're looking at the new Head of Claims for American and Shanghai."

So that was it, then, it was all about him. But when wasn't it?

"What's happening to Riley?"

No point in trying to talk to Barratt about anything else while he was full of the changes at work. She stepped back inside and let him follow her into the kitchen.

"He's going overseas for a stint," he smiled. "Which means I'm the top man, Stateside."

"That's good," she said.

He walked past her into the living room.

"You could sound a little bit more enthu—" Barrett stopped mid-sentence and sniffed the air. "Have you taken up smoking?"

"Don't be ridiculous. Of course not."

Mark was on his feet now, standing by the window, hands loosely at his sides, like a sentry, or a family retainer ready to do the master's bidding.

"So why does the room smell of smoke? Have you had someone else here? You have, haven't you? Are you having an affair?"

Ellen's head whirled.

"No! Of course not!"

But a guilty little part of her mind jumped, remembering the comforting coolness of the robot's strong shoulder against her hot, damp cheek.

"It's just, you don't seem to care very much about how I'm doing at work. And then I come back here and the house smells of smoke, so I have to wonder if you've been entertaining behind my back."

"You idiot," she glared. "As if I'd do any such thing. The only people who've been here are me and the robot. And you know the robot smokes. You bought the bloody thing."

Out of the corner of her eye, she was sure she'd seen Mark flinch, though she wasn't sure whether he was disturbed by her tone of voice, her use of the mild swear word, or her reference to him as an inanimate object.

For now, though, her attention remained on Barrett. He raised his hand and for a moment she thought he was going to come at her. She swallowed hard and tightened her arm muscles ready to defend herself. Would Mark hold Barrett off if she needed him to? Or was he constrained by his programming to support the person who paid the Corporation's bills?

She didn't find out, because after a moment Barrett drew in a slow breath and answered, "So I did." Instead of reaching for her, he put his hand to the back of the sofa and leaned on it as he unfastened first one shoelace, then the other.

Ellen exchanged a glance with Mark. Really, this exchange typified everything she'd been telling him this afternoon about her marriage. Barrett hadn't had a clue there was a problem until he came back and found her smelling of smoke. Then he'd talked himself in the space of about five seconds into believing she was having an affair, but as soon as he'd realised he'd been wrong about that, he'd settled contentedly back into blindness again. The whole episode had lasted less time than it took to smoke a cigarette.

Ellen waited until Barrett had taken off his shoes, sat down in his usual chair and turned on the vidscreen.

When she was sure the news report would drown out her words, she strolled casually towards the window and allowed herself to add in an undertone what she'd been thinking all along: "And the sad thing is, the robot is a better man than my husband."

Then she sat down on the sofa and raised her voice to ask Mark audibly, "Would you bring dinner out, please? There are steak and kidney pies in the food centre."

"Of course," Mark answered, fairly oozing obedience.

It might have just been clumsiness, because he was still learning his way around, but as he walked past, Ellen was almost certain that his hand brushed lightly across her hair.

We close our anthology with a story set in the far future, a future with Earth colonies on far-flung planets, interstellar travel, and the Circosphere — the greatest show in the universe, where entertainment is created for an entire galaxy. But for Ringmaster Jinkers Morrell, making people laugh is a serious business.

Ms Walker sent this story from London, where she lives with her family. Her stories have appeared in Lady Churhill's Rosbud Wristlet, Daily Science Fiction, and The Year's Best SF18.

Welcome to the Greatest Show in the Universe

By Deborah Walker

The flexible metal walls shrouding the Circosphere wavered as the shuttle craft drew too close. In the control booth, Jinkers Morrell sighed. "Shuttle craft…" She checked on her computer for the name of the vehicle and sighed again. "Shuttle craft *Coco the Clown*. You are in violation of the space boundary of this facility. A repeat offence will result in immediate cancellation of your free circus passes."

The spacecraft's communications array activated. Jinkers saw the faces of two teenage boys.

"Whatever happened to the famous *Amazing Galaxy Show* welcome?" asked the young pilot. He wore an illuminated clown nose. It was flashing.

"You've been notified," said Jinkers. She switched off the array and turned to Mr. Barrie, who ran the external protocols for the station. "Does that happen a lot?" she asked.

Mr Barrie was monitoring the craft on his computer, making sure that it did indeed return to the proscribed space runs. "Yes, Gaffer. A couple of times a day."

Jinkers looked over his shoulder. She was glad to see that those clowns were able to follow the route inside. "Any significance to the pattern?" she asked.

"No, Gaffer. Kids from all over the colonies like to push the boundaries."

Jinkers Morrell ran the Circosphere. She was a fine administrator. She made it her business to carry out every job on the station, at least once a year. Today, she'd been monitoring the arrival of punters and overseeing the integrity of the outer Circosphere.

"Thank you Mr. Barrie, I can see that you've got everything running smoothly here—as usual."

"Thank you, Gaffer."

Jinkers could see that he wanted to say something more. She smiled at him, giving him an opportunity to ask, "Is everything all right, Gaffer?"

To most people she would have answered, 'Sure, everything's great.' But this was Mr. Barrie. Jinkers had started her circus career here, in this control booth. So instead, she answered, "No, sir. I'm afraid not, something is wrong with my circus. I can feel it. I just don't know what it is yet."

"Aye, I thought so. I'll let you get on then."

Just telling someone made her feel better. Jinkers said her good-byes and headed back to her office.

Jinkers walked past the Theatre of Laughter where clowns played out soap-opera dramas which were televised and transmitted to the colonies. The clowns wore only tokens of their traditional dress, perhaps bright buttons on a spacesuit, or whiteface for the lead actresses. But they were still clowns attuned to the humour and pathos of the human condition. The punters packed the stalls. These actors were superstars in the colonies.

She walked past the Theatre of Culture where Earth art works were displayed. Distinguished academics waited to discuss and argue the merits of each piece.

She walked past the discretely covered Theatre of Erotica where performers danced in lavish spectacles. Jinkers smiled at the queue of youngsters waiting outside. Only those eighteen and older could enter. No one ever beat the retinal scan.

From the Theatre of Nature she heard the sounds of Earth's animals. To the punters, they were legendary beasts, seen only once in a lifetime. She listened for a moment to the roars and to the gasps of the audience. The big cats were in the theatre today.

There was so much to see here in the Circosphere, a wealth of imagination geared to every taste and desire. The best performers of Earth and her colonies were here. It was a palace of merging cultures and lavish wealth.

A flash of colour in the distance caught Jinker's eye: the gleaming tower of the Theatre of History, jewel bright against the electronic sky. Babylon had come to the Circosphere again. She remembered visiting Babylon twenty years ago, when she had first come to the Circosphere. How she'd marvelled at the sight. She had to see this again. Jinkers walked quickly to the theatre. She pushed through the punters standing at the ornate gates. The golden mosaic lions and the mushussu dragons looked down upon her.

She breathed in the aroma of the replicated Babylon: aged spice and dry sand. Costumed circus people acted out the roles of ancient Babylonians. Here were a group of Ishtar's handmaidens laughing with the punters. Here were stern faced soldiers, their eyes barely flickering as Jinkers nodded to them.

Jinkers entered the lapis lazuli palace of Nebuchadnezzar. She remembered the sense of awe that had struck her, the majesty of the spectacle that had overwhelmed her twenty years ago. There was nothing like this on her colony home world, where all resources were geared towards survival. But here on the Circosphere, there was magic. The history of Earth belonged to her and to every other human.

But now, as Jinkers walked through the palace, she didn't feel the same. She watched the punters stare in wonder at the spectacle of their collective past. She wanted to share their experience, to recapture the emotion she'd felt all those years ago. But all she could see was a facsimile of reality. When she looked at the throne, she didn't marvel at the luxury of wealth, instead she saw the cost of the gold plating and remembered the builders' overpriced estimates.

She listened to David interpreting Nebuchadnezzar's famous dreams, the dreams written into the Old Testament and passed through thousands of years of history. She saw the punters listening intently to David's words. They believed. But Jinkers only saw an actor nervously playing his first major role.

This history was only an illusion. Jinker's administrator's eye had spoiled the magic and the fantasy.

But the Theatre of History team had worked hard. She made a mental note to send a memo acknowledging their efforts. Then Jinkers left Babylon and walked slowly back to her office.

Her office was at the heart of the Circosphere. The Theatres of Entertainment ran in all directions from this core. Jinkers was responsible for the massive space station, ensuring the punters had the most marvellous time of their lives–so the real business of the Circosphere could be achieved.

A myriad messages awaited her. It was surprising how many messages could accumulate in a few short hours away from her office. She ran them through the time management A.I. programme to select for importance.

"The circus balances on a tightrope every day. That's what Barnabus Mcfee, her predecessor, used to say. But lately, Jinkers had been unsure of her footing. She felt as if the next steps she took could see the circus crashing to the ground.

The computer finished analysing the messages and prioritized a message from Brent Atwoods as the most important. She issued an e-call for him to join her immediately.

She opened the screens to her office window and took in the view. She refreshed herself in the view of the stars. Yes, it still re-energized her, even after all these years.

She took out a bowl of kibble for her pet tortoise, Horatio. She liked Horatio. *He* never did anything unexpected. And he never wandered off. He was, in fact, the perfect pet for the Circosphere administrator.

A knock on the door and Brent entered her office. He looked excited.

"Hello, Brent, what can I do for you?"

"Jinkers, you're looking well."

She wasn't, but she was grateful for his courtesy. Jinkers shared a common bond with Brent. They'd arrived at the Circosphere from the same colony world, at about the same time, both desperate to shed off the ennui of their farming colony world. They'd both risen through the ranks. They had yearned for glamour and excitement. They hadn't found it. Instead, they'd found science and administration. But dreams change as you grow older, and they were both content with their current roles. It was important work, the most important work in the galaxy.

"How's the family?" Brent was happily married to Bella, a lovely woman and a contortionist. Jinkers smiled to herself.

"Great. Great. Joshua's obsessed with the tigers at the moment."

"Wants to be an animal trainer?"

"Of course, but I'm trying to persuade him to consider veterinary science, instead."

Jinkers would have loved to have a proper conversation with Brent. It seemed that she had little time for her friends, lately. But, she thought of the all the messages on her computer and said, "Shall we get down to business? You sent me a message about some anomalous readings?"

Brent led a team of psychologists. Science and research were the real business of the Circosphere. The punters would be surprised to know that there were more scientists here than performers.

"Of course, Gaffer. There are some very interesting results from the audiences in the Theatre of Laughter."

Jinkers took the e-notepad Brent offered her. The technical data made no sense to her. "Talk me through it, please."

"It was the clowns who first noticed it. They'd been reporting for weeks that the audience "wasn't right" but we ignored them. You know how they complain." Brent scowled–a sign of his embarrassment.

"But this time?" prompted Jinkers.

"Well, they insisted. So, to humour them, we upgraded our analysis. And you know what? They were right. A significant percentage of the audience were reacting too quickly, in some cases before joke resolution."

"They were laughing before the joke? It wasn't just randomised humour?"

"No, we factored that out. There is definite evidence of pre-laughter."

"And what world has it come from?"

"It's randomised across all the colonies."

"And you interpret the data as…?"

"Some of the audience have developed precognitive ability."

"But it's randomised, right? Across all the colonies?"

Earth Central funded the Circosphere, and Earth Central feared diversity. Who could tell what strange effects the different colony biospheres might have? A different sun, strange radiation, a variation in elemental chemistry, anything might initiate physical or mental changes in the colonists. The Circosphere had two functions. To unite the colonists through a central culture, reminding them of their shared heritage; and to monitor the colonists, to check that they weren't growing away from the common core of humanity.

"I think that you can anticipate a very large increase in your research grant when Earth Central hears about this." said Jinkers. Was this the source of her strange worries? Was she sensing this change in the punters' abilities?

"Thanks, Jinkers," said Brent. He looked pleased, as well he might. This was an immeasurably significant piece of research. It certainly justified the astronomical expense of running the Circosphere. Resources and prestige would follow in the wake of this discovery.

"Bella wants to know if you want to come to dinner tonight."

"Great. Set it up with my secretary."

Jinkers worked through the rest of the reports. There were changes in the food preferences in sector six. That needed to be monitored, changes in colony preferences was important information for Earth Central's massive distribution centres. But she couldn't concentrate on her work. Her mind kept returning to Brent's discovery. Precognitive development in the punters? She felt dizzy, as though she was standing at the edge of a precipice. She wrote out her report and e-posted it to Earth Central. Who would have dreamed that humanity stood on the threshold of such an amazing development?

Dreams. For the last few weeks, Jinkers had been plagued by strange dreams. Dreams of wandering down long tunnels, looking through glass walls to see a spiral stairway reaching to the stars. She pulled up a report from the dream scientist team. Yes, there *had* been changes in the frequency and quality of the dreams in both staff and the punters. But instead of calling in the scientists for a detailed report, Jinkers decided upon a somewhat less orthodox approach.

"Got to look my best for this visit," she said to Horatio, as she pulled out a mirror from her desk drawer. She applied some skin brightening moisturiser and a natural coloured lipstick. "Not that I can compete with her. Say, Horatio, how do I look?"

But aesthetic judgements were not within the ken of her pet, and he only responded to her question with his reptilian gaze, before returning his attention to the view of the stars.

"You're not much help." Judging for herself in the mirror, Jinkers announced "You'll do," before striding out of her office to seek out the mystery of dreams within the tent of Madam Zelda.

———————

Zelda had the kind of beauty that made men sigh and women grimace in despair. She wasn't young, but she was youthful, growing inexplicably more attractive with age. And, rather annoyingly, she was a lovely person, too.

Zelda was a dream reader and fortuneteller. Brent told Jinkers that she merely read the body language of the punters. And Jinkers believed that, but in the presence of Zelda, that knowledge seemed to fade. Zelda commanded you to believe in her magic.

"Jinkers, how lovely to see you. It's been too long. How's Horatio?" Zelda invariably asked after her pet.

"It's lovely to see you, too, Zelda. Horatio's okay. He's been off his food, lately."

"He senses the trouble in the Circosphere. Wise creatures, the reptiles, old creatures."

Jinkers raised an eyebrow. "What do you know, Zelda?"

"There have many strange dreams lately. Sit down, my dear. Let me read your fortune for you."

Jinkers reached for the pack of cards that rested on the table between them.

Zelda, put her hand over the cards. "No, not those. I think the situation calls for something different." She reached for a different, older pack of cards. "These were my grandmother's cards."

"What's wrong with the other ones?" asked Jinkers.

"Choose three cards, my dear."

Jinkers moved her hand over the old, worn cards, and then quickly laid three cards on the table. She had selected, The Stranger, The Sideshow and The Void.

Zelda stared at the cards. She had lost some of her poise. For the first time Jinkers could see age resting in her friend's face.

"What's wrong, Zelda?"

"Dreams have been touching many minds lately. It betokens something, something extraordinary." Zelda smiled. "The cards are unclear, as they always are, my dear. But I will say this to you: look underneath the surface of your problems. There are unseen layers in our universe."

"I'd hoped for something a little more specific, Zelda."

"Don't worry, Jinkers. The answers will come to you soon. Use the motif of the circus to unwind them."

It was time to go to dinner with Brent and his family. Jinkers noticed that Horatio had still not finished his kibble. "What's a matter, Horatio? Do you sense it too? Zelda said that you're wise. Can you help me?"

But Horatio only stared at the window and at the distant stars.

"Something's wrong in the Circosphere, Horatio. What is it?"

Jinkers should have felt invigorated by the news of Brent's discovery, but all she felt was weariness. Perhaps she had been here too long. She was a thirty-five year old woman talking to a tortoise. She realised, with some surprise, that she was unhappy. She had friends; she had important work: the most important work in the galaxy. So why did the Circosphere feel so dull and routine? Even in the midst of this latest crisis, time felt dead to her. The magic of the circus had faded for Jinkers. It was something she'd thought would never happen.

"I'm going to put on some lipstick, and I'm going to have a good time. Paint on a smile, eh, Horatio?"

* * *

"Do you still want to be an animal trainer, Josh?" Jinkers asked. Sometimes the old tricks worked. She was enjoying herself, a home-cooked meal, the company of Brent and Bella and their irrepressible son, Josh.

"No way, Aunty Jinkers, I want to be a scientist."

"He had the revelations programme at school this week," said Bella. When the circus children turned fourteen, certain realities of the Circosphere were explained.

"Yep. I want to spy on the punters, the suckers."

"I'm not sure that's what we do here," said Jinkers, smiling. That was pretty much her own response when she had learnt about the evaluation programmes.

"It's not spying, you know that" said Bella. "There's no secret that we gather data here. We just don't advertise the fact. People come here to enjoy themselves, and if we gather some useful information at the same time, well, that's all to the good."

Joshua scowled.

He looks so much like his father, thought Jinkers.

"Aww, Mum…"

"But a scientist is a fine career choice," said Brent.

"Better pay than a lion tamer," said Jinkers.

"Well, I don't just want to be a scientist. I want to be a super scientist."

"What do you mean, Josh?"

"I want to spy on the observers, make sure that they're doing their job properly."

Jinkers laughed. "A super spy! Marvellous! Did you think that up by yourself? I wouldn't be surprised if Earth Central did have some spies, as you put it, observing us. Who watches the watchers? What's the harm if…?" She stopped, suddenly. "Excuse me. I'm so sorry, Bella, I need to get to my office immediately." Jinkers ran out of the room and sprinted to her office. She sat at her desk, panting, out of breath.

Before she did anything she needed to think. She needed to think carefully.

Jinkers believed in the ethos of the Circosphere, it was imperative to pull the colony worlds together. The Circosphere created the cohesions humanity needed to prevent fragmentation and division. Jinkers believed in science; she believed that the colonies needed to be observed and monitored.

But she also believed in the life of the circus. She pulled together all the strands of entertainment. She was the Ringmaster. She was in control of this enormous, multi-stranded palace of observation, of science, of cohesion, of entertainment and of magic. It was her circus. She was the circus. And she knew then, that somebody had got in under the canvas.

Jinkers Morrell said in a clear, distinct voice, "I know you're here – show yourself."

Nothing happened.

"Okay then," she activated her computer. "Have it your own way. I'm reporting this to Earth Central."

"Wait." A figure materialised in front of her: a humanoid figure: an alien figure.

"Who the hell are you? How long have you been in my circus?" This was big. This was massive.

"Apologies, Madam Morrell. We are representatives. We have been in your establishment for a few weeks."

"Where are you from?"

The alien walked around her office. He looked almost human, but not quite. There was an indefinable essence of strangeness cast over his entire countenance. "We inhabit another galaxy, Madam Morrell."

Another galaxy! Earth Central had dismissed the possibility of sentient alien life in the universe.

The alien continued to traverse her office. Jinkers mind was racing. He didn't *seem* belligerent. Jinker was riding along her instincts. They had always served her well.

"We are impressed that you identified us so quickly." The alien picked up a handful of Horatio's kibble. "There are always a few inconsistencies, no matter how hard we try to blend in. I'm afraid we've caused some false readings in your data. Were you expecting us? We were under the belief that your species had dismissed alternative sentience as an implausible possibility."

"This is my circus," said Jinkers "I know what goes on here. Why are you here?"

"We do the same as you, Madam. We observe. What did you say, earlier?" he smiled, an unfortunate occurrence revealing a mouthful of teeth. "Who watches the watchers? Well, we do." He held out his hand to Horatio who stretched his neck out and began to nibble the food in the alien's outstretched palm. "And Madam Morrell, to extend your metaphor: I have a free pass for you and your fellow beings to an outstanding show."

"A universal spectacular?" asked Jinkers

"Indeed. Madam Morrell, welcome to the greatest show of your life: the Universal Federation of Sentience." Horatio continued to feed. "We thought that you might like to be the one to announce the news to the rest of humanity."

The universe just got interesting thought Jinkers, as she put the call through to Earth Central.

About This Book

The typeface in this book is 11.5 Garamond and Helvetica (for the headings). It was laid out using Adobe InDesign software and converted to PDF for uploading to the printing facility.

About Darkhouse Books

Darkhouse Books is dedicated to publishing entertaining fiction, primarily in the mystery and science fiction field. Darkhouse Books is located in Niles, California, an inadvertently-preserved, 120 year old, one-sided, railtown, forty miles from San Francisco. Further information may be obtained by visiting our website at www.darkhousebooks.com.